A Novel

The Poet's Daughter

PAPER FOREST PRESS

C. K. McADAM

Contents

For my girls...

"For the nature of women is closely allied to art."
Johann Wolfgang von Goethe

Holy Roman Empire
(Around 1800)

Preface

Johann Wolfgang von Goethe has been a presence in my life since my earliest youth. For the first three years of my life, I lived on Goethe Street in the village where I grew up. For seven years, I went to a school named after the poet. Since my village was only an hour and a half from Weimar where he resided for most of his life, I visited the city and Goethe's residence on the Frauenplan Square on several occasions, as well as his garden house, a gift from the duke to entice Goethe to stay in Weimar. I've been to the ducal crypt where the poet rests next to Friedrich Schiller. I have admired the collections of maps and rocks at his house — the place that features heavily in *The Poet's Daughter*. Like most German children, I had to memorize Goethe's most famous ballad "Erlking" in school and recite it in front of the class. Much like Napoleon himself, I repeatedly read and admired Goethe's epistolary novel *The Sorrows of Young Werther* and studied his most famous tragedy *Faust*, a masterpiece of world literature (a term he invented), not only in secondary school but also in college. As an undergraduate and graduate student, I examined his life and oeuvre but also the historical, cultural, and societal context from which his poems, tragedies, novels, etc. stem. As a college professor, I have taught his poetry and dramas. In my home, Tischbein's famous painting of the poet in Italy rests on my piano. All my life, I've been immersed in Goethe's life and work. I don't idolize the man, but I feel a strong and undeniable affinity. There's something oddly familiar to me when it comes to Goethe. Perhaps it's because of his enduring presence in my life.

Yet, *The Poet's Daughter* is not about Goethe or his genius. It is about Anna, a fictional illegitimate daughter that, for me, represents the "eternal feminine" as Goethe called it at the end of his *Faust. Part II*. In addition, this novel was born out of reference to women writers of his time who struggled to be heard, and whose geniuses and literary efforts were often ignored, shoved aside, or ridiculed. Women at the time were more often than not disadvantaged in education. However, it was Protestant parsons who frequently provided their daughters and female wards with an exemplary education that rivaled men's. Charlotte Brontë, Jane Austen, Madame Necker, Louise Aston, Friederike Brun, Elizabeth Carter, and Elizabeth Singer Rowe, to name a few, grew up in parsonages and received an extraordinary education from their pastor-fathers which they put to good use as writers, translators, or salonnières. In my protagonist's case, it is her grandfather, Pastor Brion, the father of Goethe's first great love Friederike Brion who educated her beyond what was offered to women at the time. *The Poet's Daughter* is an ode to women whose extraordinary education inspired and informed their writing, as exemplified by Anna. Weimar, the seat of power for a small but important duchy and a great cultural center, provided the perfect setting to explore themes of female education and ambition during a time when the sun was setting on the Holy Roman Empire and Napoleon's military campaigns changed the map of Europe. While I had to occasionally take some liberties with the timeline, the historical context as well as biographical markers in Goethe's life are based on fact and provided some of the goalposts and the framework for Anna's story. While her character is fictitious, there has historically been much speculation about Goethe possibly fathering an illegitimate child (see "On the Origins of the Gretchen-Theme in Goethe's Faust" in the bibliography). I neither support nor endorse any of these speculations. As a writer of historical fiction and a scholar of women writers from the parsonage, I enjoyed imagining and envisioning Goethe with a daughter who inherited his genius but struggled with conformity, her ambitions, and the societal expectations and limitations of being a woman and woman writer in the early nineteenth century. For authenticity and a more immersive experience for the reader, I endeavored to use the rather stilted and formal form of narration and dialogue appropriate for the period, culture, and setting.

Prologue

1771, SESSENHEIM, ALSACE

Warm, welcoming light from the windows spilled onto the yard in front of the parsonage he had frequented over the past months. A big barn stood next to it where he and his university friends had slept on their visits to the parsonage; the same barn where he had stolen a first kiss from Friedrike.

He swallowed. This would be his last visit. He tried to drink it all in, the warm country air brushing against him, the crickets chirping peacefully in the fields and meadow nearby, and the stars overhead shining brightly in the deep blue sky. The night was darker out here but more welcoming and much friendlier than in the city. In the distance, he could hear the frogs and toads croaking in the pond where he had sat with her so many sunny afternoons and evenings. The village, dominated by the parsonage with its small but beautiful garden and the parish church, was surrounded by fields and forest. It was only a few hours' ride from Strasbourg where he had just finished his studies at the university. He would miss Strasbourg, his friends, the literary circles, and the beautiful cathedral. But he knew he would miss this parsonage with its residents even more. He sighed as he slid down from his horse.

Last fall, when his studies at the university in Strasbourg had bored him immensely, he and his friend Weyland had set out to roam the countryside surrounding the city. After a day's ride, they had stumbled upon the village of Sessenheim, where the kind and hospitable parson had offered them a meal, good conversation, and a place to sleep for the night. They would return many times after that.

The parson was an intelligent and educated man with whom he had enjoyed many great debates and musings over literature, but it was the idyll and warmth of the parsonage that had brought him back time and again. And Friederike, one of the parson's three daughters. He hadn't met her until weeks later. He and Weyland had been horseback riding in the countryside not far from the village. As they rode along, they spotted two young women walking along a country alley dusted in light snow, happily chatting. Wicker baskets were swinging on their arms, full of juncus they had cut and a few scattered chestnuts they had gathered. Friederike's light, happy walk caught his eye immediately. Her young, beautiful face showed innocence and pure happiness as if she'd never had a care in the world. From that moment, he had envied her—her innocence, her happiness, even the family she had. And from that moment, he had desired nothing more than to be near her.

He had visited the parson and his family whenever he could get away from his studies. These visits to the hospitable rectory had been a balm to his soul. The idyll of the village and surrounding nature and Friederike's lovely countenance, innocence, and childlike happiness had transformed him and his poetry. She had awakened something in him that no one had before. And he had been selfish ever since. He had wooed her to make her fall in love with him. Her loving gaze, her happy nature, and her kisses had opened the floodgates of poetry. He hated himself for his recklessness, but he'd had to drink her in, all of her. He had fed on her like a greedy and starving wolf, disregarding her innocence and tender heart. Deep down, he had always known that one day he would break her heart.

When his own father back in Frankfurt had learned of his love affair, he had immediately ordered him to break it off. But he had ignored his father's wishes. How could he leave something so lovely, wholesome, and beautiful? How could he turn his back on the parson's daughter, whose heart he had won? In the last few weeks, however, a sort of boredom had settled over him once again. He knew that the kind parson and his wife thought their daughter and him as much as engaged, expecting a marriage proposal any day. And so did Friederike. He was fully aware he had engaged her affections and had been paying her attentions that had given her and her parents false hopes. The guilt had caused him to lose many a night's sleep in recent days.

Tonight, he intended to rectify the situation. He had concluded his studies, and his father had ordered him to return home to Frankfurt and prepare for the employment he had secured. He would not bring home a wife. He was in no way ready to commit to marriage.

He led his horse to the fence and swallowed hard. Tonight, he would break not only his lover's heart but also her family's, who had been so kind, welcoming, and hospitable.

With yet another sigh, this time rather audible, he tied his horse to the fence. He wouldn't spend the night as he had done so often. Not his time. Not ever again. He closed his eyes and shook his head to himself. When he opened them again, he was determined to see through what he had come to do. Tonight's visit would be short. He straightened his shoulders and strode toward the parsonage, the happy voices echoing up to him from the inside, becoming louder with every step. He cleared his throat and knocked on the front door. It swung open immediately.

"My dear Goethe. Come in, come in," the parson said. Johann took off his hat, and stepped inside, following the parson to the drawing room where, to his surprise, a couple of his acquaintances from Strasbourg were already seated. They were members of the same literary circle there. One was indeed a friend, the other, Lenz, was merely tolerable. He despised Lenz's amateur, long-winded poems. However, tonight, a flash of jealousy struck him when he saw Lenz talking to Friederike. The idyll of the parsonage, the hospitality of the parson, and his literary circle had become well known, and more young men had made their way here to seek some diversion from their studies. It wasn't only the friendly parson whose company they sought or what drew them to Sessenheim, this much Johann knew.

He found an empty seat near Friederike, who smiled at him generously. He offered her a silent nod in return.

"So quiet tonight, Goethe?" Lenz said.

"Quiet waters are deep," he gave back, trying to keep the annoyance out of his voice. Lenz was rather dull-witted and wouldn't easily pick up on his jab, but a look at the parson told him that he had. Johann lowered his eyes. He owed the parson and his family respect and gratitude. Nothing less. He straightened his shoulders and turned to Lenz. "It is good to see you here, friend."

Lenz immediately perked up. Johann tried to ignore the look of self-importance on the man's face. "Do you have any poetry to share with us tonight, Goethe?" Lenz eyes him eagerly.

"I do indeed." He had planned to give a copy of the poem to Friederike privately, but perhaps sharing it publicly would prepare them all for what was to come.

Everyone gathered around him immediately. Friederike's eyes shone in anticipation. The parson, holding a glass of wine in his hand, smiled at him with encouragement and perhaps even fatherly pride. Goethe lowered his eyes again as he unfolded the paper. Someone put a glass of wine in his hand, and he took a greedy gulp. He cleared his throat. "It's called 'Welcome and Farewell.'" He avoided looking at anyone and began to read, his voice solemn and soft, soon falling into a mesmerizing rhythm:

> *Quick throbb'd my heart: to horse! haste, haste,*
> *And lo! 'twas done with speed of light;*
> *The evening soon the world embraced,*
> *And o'er the mountains hung the night.*
> *Soon stood, in robe of mist, the oak,*
> *A tow'ring giant in his size,*
> *Where darkness through the thicket broke,*

And glared with hundred gloomy eyes.

From out a hill of clouds the moon
With mournful gaze began to peer:
The winds their soft wings flutter'd soon,
And murmur'd in mine awe-struck ear;
The night a thousand monsters made,
Yet fresh and joyous was my mind;
What fire within my veins then play'd!
What glow was in my bosom shrin'd!

I saw thee, and with tender pride
Felt thy sweet gaze pour joy on me;
While all my heart was at thy side.
And every breath I breath'd for thee.
The roseate hues that spring supplies
Were playing round thy features fair,
And love for me—ye Deities!
I hoped it, I deserved it ne'er!

But, when the morning sun return'd,
Departure filled with grief my heart:
Within thy kiss, what rapture burn'd!
But in thy look, what bitter smart!
I went—thy gaze to earth first roved
Thou follow'dst me with tearful eye:
And yet, what rapture to be loved!
And, Gods, to love—what ecstasy!

When he finished, it took him a moment to realize that his poem was greeted with utter silence. No one spoke until Lenz suddenly started clapping incessantly. "Bravo, Goethe! Stupendous!" He gave Lenz a nod of gratitude and felt a hand on his shoulder but didn't look up to see whose it was. Eventually, people around him started to praise him and his poem. He took heart and looked at Friederike next to him. Tears stood in her eyes. She wasn't smiling. When a tear started falling, she wiped at her eyes with the back of her hand and turned away from him. At that moment, he knew that she had understood the poem had been written for her.

It was soon thereafter that he claimed he needed to get back to Strasbourg. Some of those in attendance protested, including the pastor, but not Friederike. He knew there was no need to prolong the inevitable. He said his goodbyes and took great care to express his gratitude to the pastor and his wife when he took leave. They sent Friederike out with him to see him off. She agreed obediently.

The brief walk from the parsonage to the fence where he had tied his horse was silent. Neither of them spoke. Friederike's eyes didn't leave the ground in front of her. When they reached his horse and he untied it, she finally looked up at him. He smiled at her and was glad to see her smile back. It gave him the courage to draw closer to her. Without any hesitation on his part and no resistance on hers, he took her face in his hands and kissed her gently on the mouth. He lingered, not wanting to let go, knowing it was the last time he'd be that close to her.

But when she took a step back to break the kiss, he let go of her and dropped his hands. He swung up on his horse and then reached down to take her hand. She gave it to him. "Goodbye, Friederike," he said with much effort to not sound final.

"Goodbye, dear Johann." She smiled through her tears and gave him a nod of encouragement. He let go of her hand, clicked his tongue, and rode off into the night. After a few moments, and when the light from the parsonage was almost completely covered by distance and the dark of the night, he turned around. Friederike stood where he had left her, and now that she noticed he had turned around, she gave a wave. He couldn't make out the features of her face and was grateful for it. Johann had never been so tormented by the weight of his own actions. He knew she loved him, and that he was breaking her heart.

Chapter 1

1801, SESSENHEIM, ALSACE

Anna wiped her forehead with the back of her hand but then remembered the small sky-blue cotton kerchief tied around her neck. She took it off to wipe her face with it and then stuffed it into the pocket of her apron. She eyed the empty bucket by her feet and started pumping the water from the well into the pail until it flowed over. Water seeped into the cracks of the hard, dry earth. Anna picked up the heavy bucket to carry it to the house. She did so as fast as she could to get out of the heat, and because of the weight of the water-filled pail. It had been unusually hot in the last few days, but the thick stone walls of her grandfather's parsonage had kept the house pleasantly cool, at least in the cellar and on the first floor. Upstairs, where her mother lay ill and confined to the bed, the heat had become less bearable. But her mother refused to move downstairs for more reprieve from the oppressive heat that hung over their small Alsace village like a heavy woolen cloak.

Almost daily for over a week now, Anna had gone to the little pond near the parsonage to wade in its water and cool down. To avoid any potential onlookers, she had done so in the late afternoons, when the villagers had gone home after a day's work to prepare supper.

As the granddaughter of the pastor, she was held to an impossibly high standard of propriety. Indeed, it would be most unseemly for any young woman to be seen without her stockings and with her skirts hiked up, wading around with bare legs, but the matter of her birth had long made her a suspect of violating propriety. Not that Anna gave much heed to village gossip, but she was considerate of her grandfather's station and position, and she was keenly aware of her mother's past.

Anna sighed in relief when she entered the cool house. She took the bucket straight to the kitchen and filled two jugs with water. She took one of them and carried it upstairs. In front of one of the bedrooms, she paused for a moment to listen intently. No sound came from the room.

She must be sleeping again, Anna thought. She knocked nevertheless and entered when she heard her mother's faint "come in."

Her mother greeted her with a smile that seemed to cost her some effort. Anna returned the smile and poured the fresh cool water into a cup. She noticed a sour smell and went to open the window. Her mother stood in desperate need of a bath. Anna sat down beside her mother and wiped her forehead with a cloth. "How about I draw you a bath this evening?" Anna asked.

"That would be most delightful. This heat. The bath will do me some good."

Anna was glad her mother agreed. Fresh linens would be needed, too. She sighed and avoided looking at her mother's frail body which lay exposed without a blanket to cover her. "You need to move downstairs for the time being, Mother," Anna said, trying to keep any notions of impatience out of her voice. "It is sweltering up here. You must think of your health."

Her mother tightened her lips and turned away from her as if hurt. Anna knew her mother already felt like a burden, so she quickly changed the topic. "Which herbs and flowers would you like me to add to your bath?"

Her mother turned back around to her, a smile playing on her lips. "The lavender from the garden, dear. It helps me sleep." Anna nodded and squeezed her mother's hand. "I will let you rest now and draw your bath this evening before bedtime. Please join us for supper downstairs tonight. Please?"

"Yes, I shall do so," her mother said with a cough that belied the sudden strength in her voice. Anna studied her mother's face and wondered what had prompted her resolve. Her mother always refused to come downstairs and preferred to take her supper on a tray sitting up in her bed like she did with all the other meals. And Anna understood. Her mother was just too weak to manage much more, and it took her days to recover from all the exertion if she did manage to get her out of bed.

Her mother had been bedridden for months now. She was not improving but rather wasting away. The doctor, a university friend of her grandfather's, had come by a couple of times to let blood and leave some tinctures. But there was no improvement. Consumption was uncurable, the doctor had quietly told her and her grandfather. She squeezed her mother's hand and stood up. "I will see to supper now." Her mother gave her a faint nod and then turned her gaze toward the window where a mild breeze fluttered the curtains like the ocean wind the sails.

Anna went back to the kitchen, took the second water jug, and carried it to her grandfather's study, her favorite room in the parsonage. Here she had been instructed by the old man since the age of three when he had taught her how to read. Many subjects had followed. The study was a place of learning, a library, and when her grandfather wasn't home, a space where she could write—something she had discovered she enjoyed even more than reading. She knocked and entered the room. The old man was bent over a book behind his desk. "*Grātiās tibi agō*," he said absent-mindedly in Latin when Anna poured water into his cup. He took a long draw without lifting his eyes off the book. He then put the cup back down with a satisfied grunt and glanced at Anna. "I'm glad you're here, child. I have something to discuss with you. You have read Lessing, have you not?"

"Of course, I have. All of his works. Per your recommendation," Anna said with a smile. "But I must prepare supper now. Perhaps later this evening?"

"Supper can wait a few moments longer, can it not?"

Anna laughed. She very much preferred discussing literature and philosophy with her pastor grandfather, but she could not neglect her duties either. But as usual, she gladly gave in to his request. "Supper shall have to wait then." She craned her neck to look over his shoulder at the book in front of him. "Ah, *Nathan the Wise*. A drama I know you hold in great esteem." He grunted in acknowledgment. Anna knew the play well. She had read it at least a handful of times. It advocated religious tolerance and taught that virtue transcended the differences between Christianity, Islam, and Judaism. She rested her hand on the old man's shoulder. "Is it perhaps a matter of religion that you like to discuss?"

"Indeed, it is. The perceptions of your mind are as sharp as always, my dear." Her grandfather patted her hand.

Anna began to pace around the study, listening intently to the pastor's explications. "Does not man's strength lie in his faith? In his religion?" her grandfather asked.

Anna stopped pacing, thought for a moment, and then continued walking about. "It does indeed, Grandfather. However, does Lessing not, through Nathan—a Jew nevertheless—equate true religion with morality?"

"So he does, my dear."

"And isn't woman the paragon of morality? Man does not merely hold a woman in high esteem, but particularly a moral woman. It is morality he intends to preserve in *her* for the purpose of making him a better man, is it not? Therein lies man's strength."

Her grandfather's worn face broadened. He leaned forward in his chair. The palms of both his hands rested on the open book before him. "You are quite right, my dear. Lessing speaks of morality and pleads for tolerance. A tolerant man is a moral man. Lessing was born the son of a pastor, you might remember. Nathan teaches that no religion is above the other. Not that of the Christian, of the Muslim, nor of the Jew." The old man looked thoughtfully at the book in front of him. Then he cocked his head to the side. "So, man's strength lies in his morality rather than his religion." He rubbed his chin, and his brows furrowed.

Anna could see how this realization would occupy his thoughts for a while. *And troubling thoughts as such for a pastor*, she thought. She cleared her throat to get his attention. "So, it is not so much *what* you believe but rather *how* and *why* you believe that's truly important?" Anna mused.

For a moment, her grandfather looked at her wide-eyed but then broke out into a smile. "*Exactement*. Lessing's thoughts precisely. I have taught you well, my child."

"You have indeed, dear Grandpapa." She went over to him and poured more water into his cup. "I suspect you won't share your musings in your sermon this Sunday," Anna said with a twinkle in her eye.

"Ha," her grandfather exclaimed and turned back to his book.

"I will see to supper now," Anna said. The old man muttered a reply, but it was inaudible. His mind was already occupied with something else.

Anna had prepared a plain light vegetable soup and sliced up the bread she had baked that morning. After helping her mother down the stairs so she could join them for supper, she had propped her up with pillows, so she'd be able to sit up comfortably. Anna smiled at her mother across the table from her. She looked frail and was eating so slowly, but she was eating *with* them. It had been weeks since her mother had joined them for any meal. Maybe her health was improving. It had to be. It was painful to watch her mother suffer like that, and Anna wished there was more she could do to make her mother get better.

They ate quietly for most of the meal, with her grandfather occasionally relaying some news from the village that had come to him. When the pastor mentioned he would now conduct his sermons in French, Anna gaped at him. Who would understand him? Though technically a part of France, they were Alsatian; Asatians spoke a dialect of German. When she voiced her concern, her grandfather explained that under Napoleon's rule, the French government was eager to see the French language take root in Alsace, urging it to be spoken not just in schools, but also within the walls of their churches. French had been the official language of administration and law since Alsace became part of France through the Treaty of Westphalia in 1648. Napoleon's government sought to strengthen the unity of the French state, which included promoting the French language as a unifying national language. The goal was to integrate Alsatians more fully into the French nation. Her grandfather reminded her that compliance would demonstrate appreciation for the recent concordat, an agreement between Napoleon Bonaparte and the Roman Catholic Church, which recognized Catholicism as the majority religion in France while ensuring and maintaining religious tolerance for Protestants and Jews. While the south of Alsace was dominantly Catholic, Alsatians in the north were Lutheran, like in their village of Sessenheim. Her grandfather said that he was only trying to keep Alsatians in good standing and safe from any persecution inflicted upon those who did not support the agenda of Napoleon's new government. Anna knew her grandfather was right, of course, but preaching in French would certainly not be welcomed in the Sessenheim church. Surely, her grandfather would revert back to German soon after he shared his first French sermon.

At the end of the meal, the pastor asked Anna and her mother to follow him to the parlor. A most unusual request. Anna insisted on clearing the table first. She watched the old man out of the corner of her eye, wondering why he had summoned them. Anna was surprised when her mother didn't excuse herself to retreat to her room. She could see the exhaustion etched on her face, her eyes heavy, shoulders sagging. When Anna offered to help her upstairs, her mother shook her head and, with a weak smile, followed the pastor into the drawing room. Anna hurriedly took the dishes to the kitchen with apprehensive curiosity.

When Anna arrived in the parlor, her mother and grandfather were already seated. Their eyes greeted her with studied concentration. The pastor motioned for her to sit down. Perhaps he wanted to read to them, but Anna sensed a tension in the air, thick and oppressive, much like the heat outside. For a moment she wondered if she was imagining it but her quickened pulse and cold hands despite the warmth of the room told her otherwise. An uneasy feeling had slithered into her chest the moment she had crossed the threshold. Something seemed wrong—deeply, undeniably wrong. Reluctantly, she sat down on the green settee next to her mother while her grandfather was seated in one of the armchairs usually reserved for guests who frequented the house.

To her surprise, it was her mother who spoke first. "It concerns your father..." she said, her voice measured but strained.

For a moment, Anna's heart ceased. She noticed her grandfather shifting uncomfortably in his chair. "What of my father?" Anna asked, her throat tightening. Why now, after so many years of silence and unanswered questions did her mother speak of him? The man had never been more than a shadow, a name left unspoken. She had always been told that he had left before she was born. He had left her mother and her with only the weight of his absence.

Her mother drew a breath, her hands trembling slightly. "I have written to him."

Anna felt her heart stop. The words stumbled out, half-strangled. "Why would you—?" She turned to her grandfather, searching his face for answers, but his gaze remained fixed on his daughter, his expression tight with unease, as though he too had borne the burden of this knowledge in silence for far too long.

Her mother's voice grew softer, faltering as she spoke. "Your father never knew I was with child when he left. I never told him."

Anna's world shifted beneath her feet, the room seeming to close in. How often she had tried to picture her father and yearned to see his face. But he had not even known of her existence. And now, after all this time, her mother had written to him. The very thought left her breathless, the weight of it pressing down on her like the hot, heavy air before a summer storm. "But why did you keep this from him?" Anna shook her head. "Why have you kept this from me?" Anger surged through Anna, hot and undeniable. She fought to steady her breath, each inhale trembling as she struggled for composure. All these years of silence, of unanswered questions, and buried truths. And then Anna remembered that her mother had not explained why she had written to her father. "Why, after all this time, would you write to him?"

"To tell him he has a daughter. And to—"

Anna gasped and shot out of her chair. She started pacing, her head spinning. Long ago, she had reconciled herself to the fact that her father would never be a part of her life. He had existed in a world outside of her own, flown into the ether, someone to be mourned. But how could she mourn someone she'd never met, and as she had just found out, who had never known she even existed. Her grandfather had filled the father role remarkably well, so she had not allowed herself to acknowledge the void she had occasionally felt. Now her father knew of her—knew that he had a daughter. She wondered how he had greeted this unexpected news. Anna stared at her mother who had lowered her gaze and locked her eyes on her frail hands resting in her lap. Her breathing became labored. Anna's anger vanished instantaneously. "Let me help you upstairs. You need your rest, Mother."

"I'm fine, child," her mother's breath was still ragged and uneven.

The pastor cleared his throat and spoke in a deliberate tone. "You're nearing nine and twenty of age, Anna, and remain unwed." Anna was quite taken aback by the unexpected turn in their conversation and by the urgency in her grandfather's voice. Her lips tightened. Her grandfather's words stung. She was fully aware of her situation and hardly needed any reminding. She had turned eighteen almost eleven years ago, and suiters had been few. In the last three years, they had stopped calling entirely. Her grandfather's station should have ensured her an acceptable match, particularly one with a pastor's son, but no proposals had come. She was often admired for her beauty but in the end, it was the questions surrounding her birth that had held suitors back from making an offer of marriage. The stain of being the illegitimate child of a pastor's daughter could not be plotted out. It had marked her for life.

Anna looked from her grandfather to her mother and back. "I don't understand. What does this have to do with what you just told me about my father?" The pastor motioned for her to sit once more. With reluctance, Anna returned to her place on the velvety settee. "I know I'm past the age of marriage and I have become a burden to you. Grandfather, if you would help me find and secure a position as governess somewhere close by so I can still be of help to Mother and you..."

"Become a governess?" Her mother looked at her in surprise.

"I will wait until you're better, of course. When you are fully recovered—"

"You've given up on marriage, child?" her grandfather interrupted.

"You said so yourself, Grandfather. I'm eight and twenty years of age and as of today, no one has proposed marriage. I have no prospects. But you, grandfather, have given me something far more, something more precious. An education. More than any woman could ever hope—"

Anna fell silent when the parson put up his hand. "Anna, you cannot give up on finding a suitable match. Your mother and I certainly have not." Anna wanted to speak, but a look at her grandfather told her to hold her tongue. "Your mother sent a letter to your father, not only informing him of your existence but also inquiring if you could come to live with him in Weimar for a while. There you shall have better marriage prospects due to your father's good name and influence, and where no one is aware of the illegitimacy of your birth."

Anna just stared at him for a moment. "You want me to leave? To live with a man I don't even know? Grandfather! You cannot—"

"It's been decided, child." Her mother's weakened voice was as stern as her grandfather's face.

"How can you send me away like this? To a stranger's house?" Anna got up. She was fuming and refused to hide the betrayal she felt. How could they send her away? Her grandfather and especially her mother needed her. And matrimony did not appeal to her. "Who is this man whose good name you have been keeping from me?"

"Well, you have heard of him." Her grandfather stood up, came up to her, and placed a hand on her shoulder. Then he cleared his throat and took a deep breath. "Your father is Johann Wolfgang von Goethe."

Anna stared at her grandfather in utter disbelief. She stumbled backward and then plopped back on the settee. "Goethe?!" She slowly turned her head toward her mother and looked at her in a mixture of amazement, bewilderment, and shock. Her mother and Goethe. It couldn't be. She vehemently shook her head at the thought.

She had loved everything she had ever read by him. Was the affinity she had always felt when reading his works tied to the fact that she was his daughter? Did her love of writing stem from his loins? She had devoured most of his work. His famed *Sufferings of*

Young Werther. She had read it so many times she had lost count. His dramas. *Götz von Berlichingen*. His poems. "Heidenröslein," one of the poems in a collection he had named after their village, his Sessenheim songs. Her grandfather had proudly recounted Goethe's visits to the parsonage. He had discussed these very poems with her. They spoke of love. Found and lost.

She stared at the old man, mouth open. Her stare went from her grandfather to the feeble woman next to her on the settee. "Mother—"

Anna watched her mother's far-off gaze and placed a hand gently on hers. "Why did you not tell him you were with child?"

Her mother looked at her, tears in her eyes. "I knew he was meant for greatness. And he was restless. Once he had concluded his studies in Strasbourg, his father summoned him home. When he left, I did not know I was with child. Neither did I expect to never see him again." Her mother sniffed and dabbed her face with a kerchief. She sucked in air deeply and a fit of cough followed. Anna brought her some water and her mother proceeded to speak as soon as she had controlled her coughing. But the coughing fit had taken everything out of her. Anna noticed a gurgle in her breaths now, but her mother insisted on continuing.

"Weeks after he'd left, I received a letter. He explained that he would not be returning." Her mother paused to catch her breath. "I wrote to him and told him how I felt, how unhappy it made me, but he never replied." Her mother swallowed hard. "So, your grandparents and I decided that it would be best to keep my... my condition from him."

Anna's heart ached for her mother. Goethe had not only shattered her heart but had also left her utterly desolate and ruined. Anna shook her head vehemently. "I will not live with him. I cannot. How can you insist on living with a man who dishonored a young woman like that?" She looked at her grandfather. "A man void of morality, and who did neither honor nor protect my mother's virtue."

The old man flinched, but then he pulled a letter from his waistcoat and held it out to Anna. "I want you to read it. It is from him."

Anna stared at the paper in her grandfather's hand. A letter from the great Goethe. For her. He was her father. Her ears began to ring, and she had to catch her breath. She got up and tried to steady herself. "You must excuse me," she breathed. Ignoring the letter her grandfather still held out to her, she hurried out of the room and through the front door. She barely noticed the lingering heavy heat when she stepped outside into the waning light. Lightening was grazing the far-off horizon. The bath Anna had promised her mother was forgotten. Anna ignored the signs of the approaching thunderstorm and hastened across the yard and through the gate toward the stormy clouds.

Chapter 2

1801 WEIMAR, DUCHY OF SAXE-WEIMAR-EISENACH

Johann Geist put down the quill and blew into his stiff fingers, which were stained with black ink. He briefly looked up from the papers in front of him, then craned his neck to let his eyes drift outside the window, across the square in front of his master's house. The cobblestoned square and adjoining street were lined with fine houses. The bright sunlight gave the wet stone a glaze. A horse-drawn carriage drove past, and passersby hurried along in the morning cold. He shivered involuntarily as his eyes fell on the patches of the first snow of winter, covering the cobblestones in the corners of the square and along the sides of the street. He noticed a man approaching the house, and his eyes widened. With a swift movement, he got up from the wooden chair and pushed it back in a calculated manner that would ensure it wouldn't tip over. He hastened out of the room and down the stairs.

To his annoyance, Erhart, his master's old servant, had been faster and was already opening the front door. *How did he get there before me?* Geist asked himself. He must have waited for the postman by the door. They had both been there when his master had ordered the postmaster to make sure any letters from this sender were to be delivered to the house immediately and directly to him. Geist swallowed his disdain at the sight of Erhart's shabby, patched-up suit and the greasy thinning hair as the postman placed a letter in the old man's hand. Erhart didn't as much as glance at it but shut the front door without another word, his face showing an indifference that only a man void of any ambitions and mental curiosity could muster. Geist was met with that same indifference. Erhart turned around and shuffled past him toward the staircase as if he didn't exist. With the rapid strides of the young and eager, Geist caught up with Erhart and snatched the letter out of his hand. "Thank you, Erhart, but I will deliver the letter to him." The old man's face darkened, but he didn't protest.

Climbing up the stairs, Geist inspected the handwriting and seal of the letter with singular attention. He needed to make sure his master would get it right away and that he was there when he opened it. The happy chatter of women working in the kitchen reached him once he had made it to the landing. He slowed his steps. Would they notice him walking past? He had to make sure they didn't. He held his next step and peered inside the kitchen. Two women, flour all over their hands and aprons and smudges of it on their faces where they must have brushed aside some pesky hairs or wiped off sweat, stood bent over a table, kneading dough. They didn't seem to have noticed him. He was careful not to come into view, but they looked very engaged in their own task and gossip that he felt he was in no danger of being noticed.

The younger of the two, a little plump woman around thirty in age, was the mistress of the house. She warmed his master's bed, not as his wife, but as his lover and as the mother to his children, most of whom had not survived for long. Her round face and rosy cheeks attested to her health and a possible new pregnancy. Geist couldn't understand his master's attraction to this creature, who was simple-minded, lacked proper reading and writing abilities, and had no inkling of his master's great intellect and fortitude.

Careful, not to be discovered, Geist made his way past the kitchen, rounded the corner, and was now opposite the library. Numerous books, lining the wall from floor to ceiling, were visible from outside the room, where young Master August sat at a desk in front of the shelves, chewing his lip and staring blankly ahead instead of engaging with the book before him. Geist sighed at the sight of the young boy. After delivering this letter and hopefully learning of its content, he would need to see to it that his young master was devoting himself to his studies. Geist served not only as the master's scribe but was young master August's tutor as well in a great many subjects. His father would not be pleased if he fell behind in his studies and failed to show adequate progress. Geist's position rested upon the boy's mastery of his studies.

With yet another sigh, Geist made his way swiftly to his master's study. The door was slightly ajar, but he knocked, nevertheless.

"Come in."

Geist opened the door and stepped inside. His master stood with his back turned, positioned between a large desk cluttered with writing utensils, books, and papers, and the ice-crusted window through which he gazed. Geist could hear the echo of hoofbeats and carriages rising from the street beyond the small square below.

"A letter has arrived, I take it?" His master turned to face him. As he often did when home, his master was wearing a fine comfortable banyan over a partially unbuttoned dress shirt. His face was stern, but his eyes were friendly. When he was home, he did not wear his wig to cover the unruly hair that had already begun to gray. His master's eyes fell on the letter in Geist's hand. He nodded briefly and Geist proceeded to the desk where a letter opener in the form of a miniature sword lay. He took it, opened the letter, and held the opened envelope out to his master, who scrutinized it without taking it from him.

Geist had been with his master for over a year now. While his master was strict and demanded much work, Geist had felt fortunate to have secured a position with the great Johann Wolfgang von Goethe. Gratitude and pride swelled in Geist's heart every time he marveled at this stroke of good fortune. Not only was his master a personal friend of the duke but he was also one of the greatest writers, poets, and playwrights of his time. The most distinguished minds frequented Goethe's house. On a few occasions, Geist had been present when new poetry was shared or great philosophical debates ensued. Those of great stature, power, intellect, or name had come to visit the great Goethe here in Weimar. Geist would be forever grateful to his mentor, Herder, for helping him secure the position. Although the pay was modest, the work was stimulating, and Geist could use his training in the language arts and natural sciences to be of service to one of the greatest minds the German lands had ever seen.

Geist had the sneaking suspicion that Goethe had hired him because of his love for, and knowledge of, minerals. One of his master's favorite hobbies was mineralogy. Goethe collected and studied rocks, and Geist had been astounded by the collection when he first arrived. His master's own drawings adorned the walls of the study, where a few rocks from his collection, along with maps, cluttered the side tables. Ancient Roman artifacts and busts weighed down the shelves. In the corner stood a small secretary where Geist would sit to transcribe Goethe's dictations, a task he particularly enjoyed and excelled at.

"You may leave, Geist. Attend to August's studies for the rest of the day. I'll see you in the morning."

Geist clicked his heels and offered a small bow. "As you wish, sir!" He added, trying to keep the disappointment out of his voice. He put the letter on the desk. Its contents would remain hidden from him for a while, but he would find out one way or another. Geist bowed again and left the study. August would not appreciate all the attention his tutor was about to offer him for the remainder of the day.

When Geist left, Goethe turned back toward the window, ignoring the opened letter on his desk. For a moment, he watched a couple in fine winter coats walk toward a carriage waiting for them on the road off the square. The woman had her arm through the man's, and his other hand was placed on her hand. When they reached the carriage, a footman opened the door, and the gentleman helped the woman into the carriage before following her in.

Goethe was surprised he didn't recognize them. Weimar, the seat of the Grand Duchy of Saxe-Weimar-Eisenach, was rather provincial compared to Frankfurt, where he had grown up, or Strasbourg and Leipzig where he had attended university. In Weimar, he usually recognized most faces after having lived here for two decades now. The Grand Duke Karl August had enticed him to move here with an offer he couldn't refuse: a ministerial position in his government. The duke, a lover and supporter of the fine arts, had become a close friend. Other notable men, such as his now friend and fellow poet Schiller, had moved to Weimar as well. The duke's court had become a mecca for literary and philosophical pursuits. The duke's soirees, which the duke's mother, the Duchess Anna Amalia, disapproved of, had occasionally gotten a bit out of hand but in recent years had become more polite and refined. They were no longer the young men they had been when Goethe had arrived in Weimar almost twenty years ago. Long nights filled with wine, women, poetry, and theatrics were of the past now.

He thought of Christiane, the woman he called his wife, although he had never made her an honest woman, not even after she had given birth to his children. The duke and local society would not approve of the match, although it was common knowledge that she was more than just his housekeeper. Marrying Christiane would be seen as beneath his status—an affront and an embarrassment to the duke who had granted him nobility a few years prior.

With another sigh, Goethe turned back around and sat down at his large desk. His eyes found the letter and he leaned forward to pick it up. He carefully unfolded it and began reading.

Goethe realized he had been staring at the handwriting in the letter still clutched in his hand for quite some time. The light outside was waning and his study was dipped in twilight. Erhart would soon enter to light the oil lamps. Without warning, an image entered his mind. He was not prepared for how it sent his heart racing. He quickly got up and rushed out of the room and down the semi-dark hallway into the library. Erhart had already lit the lamp in here, its light casting long shadows on the surrounding bookshelves. The library was completely deserted. August had finished his studies for the day and Geist had gone home, he assumed.

Goethe scanned the bookshelves around him. He picked up the oil lamp and held it up high to get a better look at the titles. He held it so tight, that his knuckles turned white and started to hurt. He swallowed hard, trying to keep his composure.

He hadn't seen the book in years, but it had to be in the library, on one of the shelves. His search turned more frantic as he moved from bookcase to bookcase. Then he saw it. A thin tome. Unassuming. The first edition of his first novel. He sighed in relief but took it off the shelf in haste. For a moment, he simply rested his hand on the cover. He couldn't bring himself to open it.

Then he remembered something and started thumbing through the pages with haste. He knew it had to be in there somewhere.

Suddenly, a drawing slid out from between the pages and glided onto the floor. Goethe watched it sail under the table. There it was. He had found it. He bent down and crawled halfway under the table to pick it up. Refraining from looking at it more closely, he laid it on the table in front of him and took a step back. But his eyes had a mind of their own and closed the distance he had put between himself and the picture.

It was a drawing, in his own hand, of the village parsonage that had inspired the setting for his first novel. When he was a boy, his tutor taught him how to draw with ink and pencil. As a young man at university, he had drawn everything that fascinated him and that he wanted to hold on to, to immortalize. People. Architecture. Nature. The Gothic cathedral in Strasbourg, the village parsonage of Sessenheim. But he hadn't drawn anything in a while.

Looking at the drawing in front of him, he admired the skills he once possessed. Deep in thought and not allowing his eyes to drift away from the ink, Goethe guided himself into a chair. He traced the little gate and the half-timbers on the house's facade with his fingers. He didn't realize when the oil lamp started flicking and slowly extinguishing. Only when it was perfectly dark in the library did he notice that he no longer stared at the drawing but had been exploring the parsonage in his mind's eye. Damn you, Erhart, he thought angrily. The old man had lit the oil lamp but did not realize the oil had almost been gone. He knew Erhart at times was more of a nuisance than any help, but he couldn't bring himself to let the old man go. He jumped slightly when someone suddenly rang the dinner bell. Voices from down the hallway drew nearer. He hastily seized the drawing and left the library.

When Goethe entered the dining room, Christiane and August were already seated. Christiane greeted him with a smile and August eyed him carefully. He avoided looking at them directly but simply mumbled a greeting and took his chair.

"How has your afternoon been, dear?" Christiane asked while dishing up the food.

"Fine, thank you." He replied, still avoiding looking at her. He did not want to seem discomposed. Out of the corner of his eye, he saw his son shift nervously in his chair. The boy was probably anxiously awaiting being questioned about his studies, but tonight, Goethe would refrain from doing so. His mind was preoccupied with other matters, namely the arrival of today's letter, which had unsettled him and derailed his day. Almost as much as the first letter he had received in the summer. He remembered the moment vividly—the initial shock of receiving a letter from the first woman he loved was only superseded by the content it bore. It had changed everything. And tonight, he finally had to share its contents with Christiane. Today's letter meant that he could no longer keep it from her.

The three of them ate in silence, Goethe only picking at his plate due to the growing knot in his stomach. He eventually offered August a reassuring smile to put him out of his misery. As soon as he had done so, his son began devouring the food on his plate. Goethe sighed. *I've become my father.* August was afraid to disappoint him. Goethe suspected that his son was diligent in his studies only to please him.

He noticed Christiane watching him with concerned eyes. "Everything alright?" She had stopped eating, and so had August, whose eyes had lit up with sudden curiosity, darting back and forth between his parents.

"Yes. Yes, of course, dear," Goethe said quickly and composed himself, offering her a smile to put her at ease.

"You look distraught. Has something happened?" She always noticed when something was weighing on him. She knew him well. Too well. He wasn't any good at hiding things from her.

"I... I got some news today." He put the fork down and dabbed the corner of his mouth with the cloth napkin, more out of habit than necessity.

"I hope no bad news!" She leaned back in her chair, watching him carefully.

"No. I wouldn't say so." He swallowed and noticed that August continued to let his meal get cold. He clearly sensed something interesting was about to be revealed. Goethe had always been baffled at his son's ability to pick up on other people's moods.

"Well? Will you tell me what it is about?" Christiane implored. He could tell she was growing impatient with him. Goethe looked from her to August, but Christiane didn't pick up on his silent plea for discretion. He preferred not to tell her in front of their son. She went on. "I have a proposition for you then. You will tell me about the news you received, and I will tell you what I have found out today."

Goethe furrowed his brows. "You know I'm not interested in gossip," he said, trying to keep the annoyance out of his voice. The truth was that he liked a bit of gossip now and then. Just not the kind Christiane would have to offer. He found the intrigues of the court wholly entertaining and at times amusing. And he didn't mind receiving a bit of useful information on occasion.

"No gossip. I assure you."

"What is it about then?" he asked, no longer hiding his annoyance. What was the woman going on about?

"Oh, no, Herr Goethe. You will have to tell me your news first." Christiane crossed her arms in front of her generous bosom. At least she attempted to. She was rather short, and so were her arms. She was barely able to link them. It looked quite amusing, especially when she attempted to engage him in her little games as she did now. And he loved her for it. Her innocence, her naivety, and her provincialism. It made her all the more endearing.

Goethe glanced over at August again, who was still quietly observing his parents' exchange. "You may be excused, son," he said, noticing August's disappointment as he made no attempt to hide it. Christiane looked at Goethe in surprise but proceeded to give August a nod, to which he reluctantly obeyed.

"Well, Mr. Goethe?" Christiane looked at him with big eyes, curiosity written all over her face. He could tell she fought hard to sit still and remain in her chair. She had all forgotten about supper. And so had he.

"I loved a woman once." He had said it so quietly, that he wondered if she had heard him.

"You loved a good many women, Herr Goethe," Christiane chuckled. Nothing about this was amusing, but he let her be. He needed her in good spirits. He needed her to accept what he was about to tell her.

"Let me get on with it." He shoved his chair back and stood up, glaring at her. It failed to wipe the bemusement off her face. He sighed audibly. "That woman... she wrote to me this past summer," he said, hoping she wouldn't fault him for not telling her then. "It turns out—" he swallowed and took a deep breath, "—it turns out I have a daughter." His throat constricted as he choked out the last word as saying it out loud had made it real. He had a daughter! The thought swam in his mind and invaded every space of it.

"A daughter? You have another child?" Christiane had frozen with her fork halfway between her plate and lips and stared at him. He looked on in silence as she slowly pushed her chair back to get up and clear the table. She stopped after only a moment. "Pray, what reasons have you had for withholding such news from me?" Her face had grown unusually dark. Christiane had a happy and jovial nature. Seeing her scowl at him like a she-wolf was disconcerting to say the least. "How could you not have known?" He didn't answer her. So, she proceeded to clear the table, clanking dishes loudly with no care. She was upset, that much was clear. He had expected no less. "She never told me," he defended suddenly, shrugging.

"So, you thought not telling me in turn would be the most prudent course of action?" She shook her head. "Why would she never tell you that you had a daughter?"

Goethe sat back down. "She didn't know that she was with child when I left her," he said quietly, ignoring the sudden painful tightness around his heart.

"Why did she not tell you after she gave birth then?" Christiane was relentless. She only asked questions he had already mulled over himself.

"She did not want me to marry her for the wrong reasons." He wasn't quite sure. Friederike had not revealed in her letters why she had never written him after the child was born.

"And what could possibly be the right reason if not that?" He saw how she flinched at her own words. A slow, disbelieving headshake to herself told him she understood the irony. He swallowed hard. This wasn't going the way he wanted this conversation to go.

"It's as good as any reason," she said suddenly, more to herself than to him. She stopped stacking the plates and looked at him intently. "You said you loved her." He didn't know how to respond. It was rare that Christiane outwitted him. "You loved her. You said so yourself. Just now."

"Love alone is no guarantee for a happy union." His argument fell flat, and he knew it. Christiane's childlike faith and trust in him made her typically easily persuaded; he had never lost an argument with her. Tonight, however... Christiane called him out on his cowardice, and he had no choice but to accept that he indeed had been a coward.

"But why did this woman from your past tell you now that you have a daughter?" She wouldn't leave it alone until he answered that very question.

He sighed audibly. He'd just have to come out with it. "She wants *our* daughter—" his own words surprised him yet again. "She wants her to come and live with me."

There was a moment of silence. Christiane set down the plates she had been holding in her hands and fell onto a chair. He opened his mouth to reassure her, but she shook her head. "I just don't understand. Why now? After all these years?"

"It's simple. To make a suitable match. She is living in a village as the illegitimate child of a pastor's daughter—"

"That won't earn her a suitable husband," Christiane interrupted, tracing the pattern of the tablecloth with her fingertips. She inhaled deeply.

"She has no past here in Weimar," he said.

"But she does have a father."

"It comes as much a shock to me as it does to you. All these years... and I did not know."

They both fell silent and stared at the dirty dinner dishes. The door opened and Christiane's woman servant entered to help her clear the table. Christiane let her proceed and turned to Goethe. "So, will you? Take her in?

He looked at her thoughtfully. "What would you do, my dear?"

"She is your daughter. You cannot refuse her," she said as quietly as possible. Perhaps because of the servant's presence.

"You are a good woman, Christiane. Goethe walked over to her and took her hand in his, smiling. He looked into her eyes and guided her hand to his lips to kiss it. Then he remembered her words from before their argument. "So, what news have you for me, dear?"

Christiane glanced briefly at the servant who was about to leave the dining room with a tray full of dishes. After the woman left, Christiane turned to him. "I am expecting again!" She said with a hesitant smile.

"That is indeed good news, my dear!" he said. The joy he felt was immediately crippled by fear. Fear for a miscarriage, a stillbirth, or some childhood illness that would snuff out another light he had helped bring into the world. He squeezed her hand while smiling encouragingly at her. She forced a smile, but her eyes were uneasy. "Everything will be fine this time. You'll see," he reassured. He turned away quickly after that, hoping Christiane hadn't seen the doubt in his own eyes.

Chapter 3

1802

Goethe let his eyes drink in the beautiful and familiar landscape that drew by. His carriage was rattling down the bumpy country road at a slow pace. He already regretted having Erhart drive rather than hiring a coachman who would have certainly quickened the pace. It was spring. The rain that had filled the numerous potholes had also painted the fields and meadows in beautiful yellows. Goethe had lowered the windowpane to let the fresh air into the stuffy carriage. He closed his eyes for a moment to let the air brush against his face. Although bumpy, the drive would make him fall asleep in an instant if he allowed himself. But he didn't. He couldn't. He opened his eyes again and cleared his throat.

"You do look very much like your mother," he said to the young woman across from him. Her blond braided pigtails, her youth, and the simple country dress reminded him so much of Friederike. She was a spitting image of her mother and only a few years older than when he had first met her. He couldn't detect any familiar features from his side of the family.

"So, people say," the young woman said and turned to look out the window. He followed her gaze for a moment and then brought his attention back to her. Her fine features belied her simple upbringing. Her eyes appeared cold but were of much clarity. His breath had caught in his throat when he had first laid eyes on her in the small coach inn in Strasbourg where she had waited for his arrival so he could take her to Weimar. Goethe was relieved that Pastor Brion had greeted him as an old friend.

He studied her face intently. "I didn't know about you."

She remained turned to the window but said, "Yes, I know. My mother told me."

"And did she tell you why she has sent you to live with me?" he asked.

She turned her head toward him. "That's very obvious, isn't it?" She pursed her lips and folded her arms, which made her look younger than she was. "I'm in need of a husband." Their gazes locked for a moment until she turned back toward the window.

Her tongue told him she was not only educated but was also blessed with a quick mind. She was neither timid nor shy. Different from her mother in that regard, he thought. However, her bluntness would not do in society.

He looked back outside at the forest that sprawled the landscape in the distance. It reminded him of a day when he and Friederike, dressed in the same traditional village attire as his daughter, had been picnicking in a wheat field next to a forest much like this. They had fed each other, laughed, and then kissed. They had been so very much in love. Goethe remembered her eyes that day. They were as bright as the glistening sun that had peeked through the branches of the trees overhead. How full of happiness she had been that day. And it had been infectious. He had felt the same. Never in his life before had he felt such bliss.

For a brief moment, it was as if he could still feel that bliss; the laughter still ringing in his ears, the sweet taste of her lips. But the feeling vanished as quickly as it had come over him. He shifted uncomfortably, afraid his daughter, sitting across from him, would hear his thoughts.

While the feeling had passed, the memories came flooding in powerfully. In his mind's eye, he saw himself grabbing a little book, scribbling a few lines, and then reading them to Friederike. She threw her head back, laughed, and then took the book from him. He remembered every detail. How he kept kissing her while trying to wring the book out of her hands. But she kept kissing him, too, so innocently yet so playfully that she drove him mad. She had never realized how mad she drove him. Eventually, he gave up on the book and instead made passionate love to her. He wondered if that was the moment he had fathered his daughter.

He offered the young woman across from him a smile even though she wasn't looking at him. "We will stop in Frankfurt for the night and continue our journey to Weimar in the morning," he said softly. Her head was still lowered, but she nodded. He knew this was probably difficult for her, to leave everything and everyone she had ever known behind to live in a strange city with a strange man who happened to be her father. He was putting all his hope in Christiane and August to be welcoming to her.

They had a mere hour left of their journey. As they approached Weimar, Goethe's spirits lifted in anticipation of welcoming his daughter to his home. She, on the other hand, appeared apprehensive, which he brushed aside. She would adapt to her new life quickly. He realized that he had been staring at her when she suddenly looked up at him. He cleared his throat and looked away quickly, pretending to be interested in the village outside the window he knew was only a few minutes away from the city.

Only a few moments after they had passed through the village, the country road turned into cobblestone, the ride became less bumpy, and the sound of coach wheels on stone filled the air. Soon after, the carriage slowed down and crawled along alleys. People were stepping out of the way, and some men were doffing their hats with accompanying slight bows toward them. He nodded back the occasional greeting.

He smiled to himself when he noticed his daughter gazing out the window with unmistakable curiosity. She studied the houses and people of Weimar as they passed them.

"You will like it here. I have found a home in Weimar, and so shall you," he said. She didn't respond but kept taking in the cityscape and hustle and bustle in the streets. "You will find Weimar quite diverting. It might be somewhat of a provincial town, but there's much to entertain," he added.

After the carriage had turned a corner, it came to a sudden stop. "We have arrived, it seems," he said with some excitement. She turned to him, her face unreadable. Any curiosity he had sensed before had vanished, replaced by apprehension. A moment later, Erhart opened the door of the carriage for them, and Goethe climbed out. She followed, and he helped her down himself.

This is my house," he said unnecessarily, gesturing to the building in front of them. She simply nodded, barely glancing at it, seemingly unimpressed.

Goethe led the way to the large wooden front door and paused, waiting for Erhart to open it. Once inside, he immediately heard August storming in through the back door, heading toward them. Goethe glanced at Anna, who was watching Erhart retrieve her meager luggage from the carriage.

"Papa!" August came rushing toward Goethe but came to a sudden halt in front of him. He bowed slightly. "Welcome home, Father." Goethe smiled at his son and then proceeded to tousle his hair.

Anna had observed the exchange with some curiosity. August just now noticed her presence. "Who is she?"

"Manners, August."

Anna took a step toward him. "I believe I'm your... Well, call me Anna." Goethe looked at her in surprise and then gave her a satisfied nod, glad to see her graciousness - not to mention her discretion. He hadn't seen this side of her and found it rather welcoming.

August observed her with keen interest, but much to Goethe's relief, he eventually bowed like a gentleman. "I'm August. Pleased to make your acquaintance, Anna."

"Now run along, August." They all turned to see Christiane, who had appeared out of nowhere. Beside her was her maidservant, carrying a stack of folded linens. Christiane wore a simple dress with an apron. Goethe noticed that her figure had begun to change, the tell-tale signs of her condition becoming apparent.

"You heard your mother," Goethe said.

"Yes, sir," August said with a hint of disappointment in his voice and marched back whence he had come.

Anna stepped toward Christiane and gave her a quick curtsy. "You must be Madame Goethe."

"Oh no, dear. Christiane will do just fine," she said with an amused side glance at Goethe.

Goethe brought a fist to his lips and cleared his throat to gain the women's attention. "Christiane, will you show Anna to her room? I'm sure she's exhausted from the long and arduous journey."

"Very well. Come with me, Anna." Christiane turned toward the stairs, and Anna followed her. Behind them, the maidservant kept her distance but carried the linens after them.

Goethe could hear Christiane's heavy breathing as she climbed the stairs with some effort. Halfway up, she paused and turned around to Anna. "Now tell me, dear. Is Anna your full first name?

He saw how Anna shook her head. "It is short for Johanna."

Christiane briefly peered over the handrail at him. "So, your mother named you after your father?" Christiana asked.

"I did not know who my father was until recently. She told me Johanna meant 'gift from God.' Still, I have always only been called Anna."

With this, the two women proceeded up the stairs, toward Anna's new room.

In the foyer, Erhard entered with Anna's bag. As he passed Goethe, his face showed a hint of amusement. Erhart's face was usually unreadable, something Goethe had always appreciated from him, in addition to his discretion. That's why Goethe had a hard time retiring him. With an audible exhale, Goethe watched Erhart climb the stairs with the same difficulty as Christiane before taking off his hat. He ran a hand through his hair. With another glance up the stairs, he proceeded to his study. There was enough daylight left to attend to some business and writing.

As always when he dictated, Goethe stood by the window with his arms behind his back, staring into the distance and not letting the commotion on the square and the street below distract him. Geist, his scribe, was sitting at his small secretary, waiting for him to formulate the words. Goethe cleared his throat. "One never goes so far as…" He listened intently to the soft scratches of Geist's quill that told him when to continue. "… one who doesn't know where he is going—" A soft knock on the door caused him to pause and turn. "Perhaps we should finish this letter on the morrow," he suggested.

Geist merely nodded, his agreement silent but understood, as he laid down the quill. Rising from his chair, he crossed the room and opened the door. There stood Anna, a shy smile gracing her features. She briefly met his eyes before stepping aside. Without acknowledging her further, Geist exited the room, treating her as though she were invisible.

Goethe stepped around his big desk and gestured to a chair. "Please. Please, come in and sit."

Anna entered the study, her gaze wandering with quiet curiosity. Her eyes fell on the offered chair, and she sat down. Goethe walked over to her. "Have you received any schooling?"

"My grandfather taught me," she said without looking at him. She was examining the busts on his shelves.

"Your grandfather! Excellent! A fine mind and a fine teacher." He ignored the sudden sense of loss that pierced his mind and heart. Friederike's father, the village pastor, had received a university education and been a tutor of many young men. The book selection in the pastor's study had not only impressed Goethe but everyone else who had visited the parsonage. He had fond memories of their philosophical debates.

"He taught me how to read and write from a young age. Also, French and Latin," Anna said, interrupting his thoughts.

"Ah," Goethe said, nodding. "And how is your writing?"

Anna looked at him with raised eyebrows. "My grandfather found it satisfactory."

Did he detect a sense of pride in her words? "And how do *you* find it?"

"I can write well, sir." She held his gaze. "I enjoy it very much."

"You do?" His eyes fell to her fingers, which were stained with ink. For a moment, he wondered what she was writing. Perhaps she kept a diary or engaged in frequent correspondence. It didn't matter. He was relieved to hear she had been properly educated. He had expected no less from the pastor. "Very well, then. Good writing is an essential skill. It took me months before I found my scribe Geist."

He studied her with quiet intensity. When she averted her eyes, he continued. "You ought to take better care washing the ink stains from your hands." He pointed to her fingers.

Anna glanced down, surprised, before quickly clasping her hands together to hide the traces of ink.

"To prepare you for marriage, Christiane will instruct you in needlework. I shall also find you a tutor for music and dance—"

"I have no desire to dance, sir," Anna interrupted, her voice firm. "And my mother has already taught me needlework."

Goethe's eyes widened slightly, his lips curling with faint amusement. "Very well, no dancing, then." He shifted his stance, growing more serious. "Your mother's letters spoke of how you cared for her, and how you managed your grandfather's household with diligence."

Anna narrowed her eyes. "Yes, sir. I did."

"Very well. I believe it would be best then if you helped Christiane manage my household." Anna's eyes widened. Did he notice a hint of disappointment in them? He ignored it and continued. "Especially right now. She will need help until—"

"That would be best." With a reaffirming nod, Anna got up. Too quickly, he thought.

Goethe reached for her arm but dropped his hand midway. "You will let me know if you stand in need of anything," he said gently. "Please."

Anna held his gaze for a moment as if she wanted to speak but then simply nodded and left, closing the door quietly behind her.

Chapter 4

1802

After a few weeks in Weimar and with summer approaching, Anna had started to feel more at ease in her father's house. Except for Geist, everyone had made her feel welcome. Christiane was particularly grateful for Anna helping her run the household.

Anna was chopping meat for tonight's supper and salting some pieces to preserve them for future meals. She took a break to wipe her forehead and studied Christiane's face. She was only a few years her senior but more experienced than her. Perhaps childbirth and raising children fostered a depth of maturity that couldn't be achieved through any other means. Christiane stood at the kitchen hearth across from her, stirring the soup that was cooking over the open fire. Her face was flushed from the heat of the hearth, and pearls of sweat had formed on her round face, giving her a dewy glow. Christiane noticed Anna looking at her and raised her eyebrows.

Anna smiled at her. "Would you like me to attend to the soup for a moment so you can sit?"

Christiane offered a grateful nod and sank down on a stool. "Heaven sent you to us, Anna," she said, moaning and rubbing her sore back. Anna poured her a cup of water and Christiane drank greedily. "You must miss home," Christiane said suddenly, her eyes fixed on Anna.

"I do, but you have been nothing but kind to me. It must not be without difficulty for you to have me here," Anna said quietly.

"I wager it proves far more difficult for you, my dear." Christiane got up and took the big wooden spoon out of Anna's hand. Anna went back over to the table to continue preparing the meats. She waved her hand to shoo the flies away and began chopping again, placing each piece in a stone jar and then applying salt for preservation.

Only when she saw blood trickling from the fleshy base of her left thumb did she realize she had chopped herself. With the realization came the searing pain that took her breath away, and she had to steady herself. Salt had gotten into the cut.

Christiane swung around to her and looked in horror at the angry gash. She grabbed a rag and pressed it on Anna's hand. For a moment, Anna thought she would faint.

"You sit here," Christiane said and pulled her over to the stool. I will find Erhart to fetch the doctor. With that, she rushed out of the kitchen and left Anna feeling utterly abandoned. The wound was pulsing with fervor as she watched her blood seep through the rag.

Moments later, her father and Christiane came rushing in, both seemed stricken with panic. Her father swept her up and into his arms, carrying her out of the kitchen. Her head throbbed and bile rose to her throat and then everything went black.

She must have fainted after all because the next time she came to, she was lying on her bed. Another searing pain in her hand must have woken her, and when she looked down at it, she stared in horror at a man stitching up the wound. She wanted to scream but felt Christiane's comforting hand holding hers above her head. She noticed her father standing to the side, chewing his lower lip as his eyes avoided looking at the doctor's task.

The piercing pain was replaced by an ardent throbbing when the doctor was finally done tending to her. She studied her hand, which was wrapped in linen bearing traces of her blood.

"It is of the utmost importance that the wound does not get infected," the doctor said to Goethe. "She needs to hold it absolutely still for the next two weeks."

Her father nodded and saw the doctor out.

"You will need to rest now, dear," Christiane said, leaning over to wipe Anna's forehead. "You gave your father quite a fright; he was beside himself." Christiane adjusted Anna's blanket. "And you gave *me* quite a fright. I shouldn't have asked you to chop that pork."

"This is not your fault, only mine," Anna choked out. "I've caused you much distress."

"I will hear none of it. We will make sure you're healing properly, and that's all that's important now." Christiane patted her shoulder and offered her a reassuring smile. "You rest now, dear," she said and left.

Anna surveyed the room, but it dissolved into a blur. She clenched her jaw in pain and closed her eyes. The throbbing in her hand had not let up, and she wondered how she would be able to find rest. While Christiane and her father had taken good care of her and had been nothing but kind since her arrival, she felt terribly homesick, especially now. She missed her mother and grandfather dearly, the idyll of her village, the homely parsonage, and the Alsatian food. She was grateful that they had kept her abreast of any news at home with frequent letters. Occasionally, particularly when she would help Christiane, Anna felt guilty that she could not be in Sessenheim to look after her mother. In those moments, she reminded herself that it had not been her choice to be so far from home.

She found some solace in books and in her writing whenever she retired to her room. Secretly, Anna hoped that one day her father would discuss literature with her as her grandfather had done. That he would share his writings with her and teach her to be a writer. But she was keenly aware that her father had only one goal for her. Marriage. And a proper marriage at that. To a respectable gentleman.

Anna enjoyed the slightly burning warmth of the mid-summer sun on her face as she walked. As she often did now, she found herself gently stroking the still tender base of her left thumb while otherwise occupied. The throbbing pain from her injury had long ceased and only the angry red scar that spanned from the base of her thumb to her first knuckle was a reminder of her unwitting attempt to chop meat. To everyone's great relief, she had not taken a fever in the days after it happened, and the wound had healed properly. With time, the scar would certainly lessen in appearance. At least that was what she hoped.

It was already late morning as Anna and Christiane made their way to the weekly market at the town square. Christiane walked with a gentle sway, heavy with child now. Both had wicker baskets swinging on their arms as they made their way down cobbled-stoned alleys lined with fine houses. Since it was market day, many people, from well-to-do citizens of Weimar to servants, were out doing business and running errands.

Anna noticed that only those dressed in simpler clothes greeted Christiane as they passed by. The finely dressed townspeople ignored her. Christiane did not seem to notice them. So, Anna chose to do the same.

When the big town square with the town hall and fine merchant homes opened up in front of them, the noise increased drastically. Carts, carriages, and the people of Weimar and the surrounding villages seemed to fill every empty space. Sellers cried out prices to those passing between stands. Anna stayed close behind Christiane, who maneuvered through the crowds unfazed and with a determination that surprised Anna and silenced the shouting vendors around her. In passing, Anna eyed the sellers' offerings. From pig heads to sausages, fresh carrots, beans, and cucumbers, to French port, Anna admired the plenty of it all. The weekly market in her village now seemed rather insignificant. Goethe had called Weimar provincial, but Weimar was the biggest city she had ever lived in.

Christiane interrupted Anna's gaping, calling over her shoulder. "We'll go to Herr Kurz today. His tomatoes are always fresh and juicy, and his scales don't put on any extra weight if you know what I mean."

Tomatoes. Her grandfather and mother had always regarded them with suspicion. They could not be found at their village market, and Anna had only seen them in Strasbourg. Her father seemed to have a taste for them. He had said they reminded him of Italy where he had spent two years. Tomatoes had been served at a handful of suppers since Anna had come to live with him, but she had declined them on each occasion.

Christiane didn't wait for a response from Anna and marched on at the quickest pace her protruding belly allowed. The physical toll it took was evident in Christiane's shortness of breath and odd sway which clearly indicated the difficulty of carrying a child. Anna had never been around someone this heavy with child. She promised herself that she would not find herself in that situation any time soon, let alone carry the child of a man who refused to fulfill his moral obligation. Although marriage didn't appeal to her at the moment, seeing her mother bear the burden of dishonor and endure society's ridicule had led Anna to conclude that marriage was far from the worst fate for a woman. Nevertheless, if she could help it, she would delay any prospects of a union as long as she could. She had no desire to put herself through the demands of pregnancy and the dangers of childbirth any time soon.

Christiane was breathing heavily when they arrived at Herr Kurz's stand, who recognized Christiane instantaneously and greeted them eagerly. "I already have it all ready for you, Demoiselle."

Christiane laughed heartily; a sort of belly laugh she claimed she had only developed since she had gotten pregnant. It suited her so much that Anna couldn't imagine Christiane's laugh any differently, and she smiled with genuine delight at the older woman. While Christiane lacked a proper education, she was kind and good-natured, jovial and agreeable. Anna understood why her father cherished her company. She appreciated that Christiane didn't try to mother her but treated her as an equal even though she was older, if only by seven years.

While Christiane was talking happily to Herr Kurz and inquiring about the most recent gossip, Anna wandered over to a few other stands to survey the goods. To her dismay, she saw a couple of gossiping women pointing their fingers at Christiane and her rounded belly. With furrowed brows, she returned to Christiane.

"Let me take this." Anna reached for the now filled and heavy basket and took it from Christiane while handing her the empty one.

"Bless you, my dear," Christiane said with a grateful smile. Anna returned it and linked arms with Christiane, who dropped some coins into Mr. Kurz's palm. When they passed the two women who had sneered at Christiane, Anna made sure they saw her glaring at them. They hushed their voices and turned away.

As they left the market square, Anna turned to Christiane. "Tell me about you and my father." She hoped her request was not too forward so as to offend her.

Christiane stopped walking, but she was smiling and lifted her brows in surprise. "Well, by now you will know—"

"I know that you're not married. Why?" Anna decided this was as good as any other time to get some information about the state of the household she was living in now.

Christiane sighed and began walking again. "I think you should ask your father that."

Under no circumstances did or would Anna want to ask him. Christiane was another matter. Anna had begun to trust her. And Christiane didn't mind sharing or talking about herself. So, Anna seized the opportunity to see if Christiane would answer the questions she had wanted to ask ever since she had arrived. "Why has he not proposed marriage? After all, you share a home as well as a son and—"

"Have one on the way," Christiane interrupted. She stared straight ahead and kept walking.

Anna brought them to a stop so she could face Christiane. "That seems rather enough reason, does it not?" Anna said gently.

"It does indeed." The smile had vanished from Christiane's face.

Although Christiane's mood had shifted, Anna continued. She hoped the next question would deflect from the previous one that had clearly caused Christiane pain. "Do you love him?"

Christiane eyes widened, a hint of puzzlement evident in her expression "What's there not to love about him? He took me in, and he has always been kind to me. He is the father of my child." Christiane drew closer and what she said next was almost a whisper. "And he is Johann Wolfgang von Goethe, the great poet. Of course, I love him. How could I not?" Anna was taken aback by the sincerity, but Christiane wasn't done. "And he loves me well in return. There's nothing else to it."

"I understand. I think." Anna looked ahead thoughtfully. She had more questions but felt that enough was said for the day. She linked arms with Christiane again, and they started down the street.

As they rounded the corner, the house came into view, and Anna let go of Christiane's arm to shift the heavy basket to her other hand. Then she felt Christiane's hand touch her shoulder. "There are many things I do not understand about your father, Anna. We do not have much in common, you know. He knows so much and I so very little. He's seen the world. I've never left Weimar. He's from a well-to-do family. My family on the other hand had very little money. I grew up with five siblings, and after my father lost his position, I had to work as a maid. This is how we met, you know."

"How?"

"I was sent to him with a petition for help. He had kindly listened and offered to employ me as his housekeeper. He also found my brother employment." Christiane sighed loudly. "Anna, we couldn't be more different. He's a genius while I'm but a simple woman..." Christiane trailed off and locked her eyes on the house in front of them. "But I'm certain he loves me, and this is as much as he is able to give me. It is more than I could have hoped for."

Anna followed Christiane's gaze to the stately house in front of them. She empathized with Christiane but did not want to accept the fact that her father would dishonor yet another woman by not proposing marriage when it was his duty to do so.

It was still very early in the morning when Anna made her way to her father's library. She enjoyed rising at dawn to get her tasks done when everyone, even Erhart, was still asleep. She opened the door, dusting cloth in hand, and slipped inside. She made sure to close the door quietly behind her. It was her favorite room in her father's big house. For months, she had wanted to inquire of her father if he would agree to lend her a book or two. She had yet to find the courage to do so. She scanned the big shelves that reached the ceiling and were filled to capacity with books. She set the dusting cloth aside on the big oak table in the center. While society disapproved of a woman's penchant for books and learning, Anna had sought every opportunity to read since she was a child. Her grandfather had granted her an exceptional education. While he knew it was frowned upon that he taught her beyond basic reading and writing, he had claimed that he could not accept seeing a sharp mind as hers lie dormant after she had begun reading at three years of age. In addition to the private tutoring she had received from him, he had let her join in lessons he offered the sons of well-to-do merchants and lawyers, even some of the well-to-do farmers, who wanted their heirs properly tutored so they'd be able to receive a university education and become learned men. But a learned woman? It was a rarity indeed, but her grandfather had seemed set on making her such.

And how grateful she was to him. He had let her read any book she wanted that was housed in his study. Due to his diligence, she was fluent in French and Latin and had studied the natural sciences, moral philosophy, history, and literature. Together they had studied and expounded poetry. Klopstock, Schiller, and her father's. She had devoured any book by them and had tried to emulate their writing. Not that she wanted to become a poet herself, but playing with words and committing her musings to the page brought her much enjoyment and much-needed diversion.

Yet her grandfather had steadfastly declined to instruct her in one particular subject of her choosing.

Anna moved along the shelves and let her fingers run across the book spines. Her head was cocked to the side so she could catch the title of a book here and there. Suddenly, she stopped short and held her breath. Her fingers, as if of their own accord, rested on the spine of a particular book. Her father's library did indeed hold many treasures. She felt her heart leap in excitement as she glanced back at the door, then swiftly pulled the book from the shelf. Her eyes flew across the pages. As if she had been in this library all her life, she guided herself onto a chair at the table without taking her eyes off the page.

Anna didn't know how much time had passed. She always lost track when reading. But suddenly the door swung open, and Geist stepped in, followed by August. She knew Geist hated her presence in the house. He let her feel unwelcome whenever he got the chance. Her father hadn't noticed.

Geist stopped short when he noticed Anna. She jumped up and the book fell to the floor. For a moment, he simply stared at her, but then slowly began to shake his head in disapproval. When Anna moved to pick up the book, he swiftly bent down before she could.

"I know Herr Goethe would not like to see his books treated this way," he said, his voice cold and arrogant.

"I was just—"

"Dusting?" Geist said with raised eyebrows and a sneer, side-glancing at the dust cloth on the table.

"And reading," Anna gave back. She wouldn't allow Geist the satisfaction. August smiled at her in support, and she shot him a smile back. It pleased her to let Geist know she didn't appreciate his arrogance. "Is a woman not to read, Herr Geist?" To her great pleasure, she saw that she had caught Geist by surprise.

"If she can afford the time." Geist recovered quickly and smirked at her.

"Very well. May I ask you a question then, Herr Geist?" Geist arrogantly waved his hand for Anna to proceed. "Do you consider reading leisure, Herr Geist?"

Geist looked intrigued by her question. "Certainly not for everyone... but certainly for a woman."

"Don't you agree that a woman needs to be well-read to educate and guide her children?" Anna winked at August, who suppressed a chuckle.

"Well, maybe you should take over the young Master August's lesson then," he said condescendingly.

"Maybe she should." August had stepped forward, both hands on his hips.

Geist addressed August sternly, his brows furrowed. "I was not being serious. You can't think she—this is a child's game. I won't be part of it," Geist huffed and left the library.

When Geist was gone, Anna and August smiled at each other.

"He thinks too much of himself, doesn't he?" August was laughing now. Then he looked at the book. "What book is that? The one you were reading?" August pointed at the book Geist had left on the table.

"A collection of plays by Euripides," Anna said and walked over to the book.

August raised his eyebrows. "Do you know Greek?" he asked incredulously.

"No. It's a translation."

"I have another tutor who teaches me Greek. Father doesn't allow me to read anything in translation. I have to study other languages, too. French, English, Italian, and Latin, of course."

Anna nodded absent-mindedly. Her grandfather had tutored the boys and young men of his rectory in Latin and Greek. While he had taught her much, including French and Latin, even he had considered a woman studying Greek a step too far. "I wish I could read all the great Greek plays in their original language," Anna said with an audible sigh.

"I could teach you what I learn from the tutor... if you like," August said.

"You'd do that? Why?"

"We could read together and help each other." He lowered his eyes to the ground. "The tutor is very impatient." Anna noticed how August rubbed the back of his left hand.

"We could meet here, in the library, whenever Herr Goethe is gone," she suggested. "I don't think he would approve if he discovered a woman studying Greek."

"And when he's not engaged in his many travels, he's dictating in his study. Geist will be with him then, too, so we can have the library all to ourselves," August said conspiratorially. "Should we shake on it?" With that, he stretched forth his hand. Anna grinned. She liked August and was grateful he had accepted her into the household. She took his hand, and they shook. "I will have to find where Geist stormed off to now, I fear," August said. "I do need my lessons. Father would not approve," he sighed and started for the door.

"Good luck," Anna said. With a sigh, she carefully picked up her discarded book of plays and looked for the empty space on the shelf where she had found it.

"I'm sure Father won't mind," August said motioning to the book before he disappeared through the door.

Anna smiled after him and, after a moment of thought, set the book back on the table. She grabbed the dust cloth and proceeded to wipe down the shelves. This time, she avoided reading the spines of the books. Her thoughts were buried in Euripides' plays. She had always favored plays over poetry. Her grandfather had referenced them on a few occasions, but he himself had never had the opportunity to read them. One day, she would be able to read them. In Greek. The anticipation made her flush and she hurried to finish dusting.

Anna watched in confusion as Christiane hurried back and forth in the kitchen, which was quite concerning in her delicate and advanced state. Her pregnant belly bumped occasionally into this or that, and she looked flustered. Anna had never seen her so out of sorts before. The water before Anna began to boil, and she carefully poured it into the teapot, just as Christiane had instructed her.

After everything for tea had been arranged on a tray, Christiane seemed to settle down, quite literally sighing in relief. "Everything seems in order. Good." She turned to Anna. "Go on! You will serve the tea to his guests."

"But—" Anna wanted to protest, but Christiane cut her off.

"He does not like me to come out while he has visitors."

"They don't know about you?"

"Well... they do," she said, brushing down her skirt. She went over and started to untie Anna's apron. "You know, it's not appropriate for me to live with him. People don't approve." She took the tray and held it out to Anna. "Please, Anna. You'll do it for me, yes?"

Anna felt for Christiane. How could she deny her request? She took the tray out of Christiane's hands, who nodded in gratitude, and then left the kitchen, tray in hand and ready to serve her father's guests.

Anna knocked softly on the closed door to the parlor, which was reserved for visitors.

"Come in." It was her father's voice. Anna pushed the door handle down with her elbow, taking good care not to spill any tea. She slid inside the comfortable space. A small round table with chairs for tea, a chaise longue off to the side, and a couple of cushioned wooden chairs with bright blue elegant fabrics to accommodate more relaxed conversation furnished the room. Paintings of ancient mythology adorned the papered walls. The statue of one of the Roman Caesars stood in one corner of the room.

Around the table sat her father, another gentleman near his age, and a lady a few years older than the two men but still, very beautiful.

Her father, who usually wore his banyan around the house, was dressed in a fine tan waistcoat. He looked at her with raised eyebrows as if he hadn't expected her. He seemed to collect himself quickly, got up, and made room for her to set down the tray. He smiled encouragingly, so she placed the teacups in front of the visitors and poured the tea.

"Thank you," Goethe said to her. Then he turned to his guests. "My dear friends, if I may introduce to you... this is Anna." Her father raised his eyebrows expectantly, so Anna curtsied to his visitors. "Anna, these are my dear friends Frau von Stein and Herr von Bendeleben."

"Charming," the lady said and gave her a nod in return for the curtsy.

The gentleman stood. "Pleased to make your acquaintance, Demoiselle." He smiled kindly at her and gave a quick bow.

"Anna is the daughter of an old friend from Strasbourg. She will stay with us for a while."

Anna froze. She stared at her father, who pretended not to see her reaction. Then she briefly looked to the side to swallow down the hurt and gain her composure, hoping her father's visitors hadn't noticed. Why had he not acknowledged her as his daughter?

"Please, have some tea," Goethe said to his guests and motioned to Herr von Bendeleben to sit back down.

Anna realized she was dismissed. With another curtsy, she took the tray. Herr von Bendeleben stood back up and bowed to her. "Very pleased to have made your acquaintance, Miss Anna." Without looking at any of them, especially not her father, Anna left the parlor.

Goethe shouldn't have been surprised that Anna had brought in the tea. Christiane hated the coldness with which she was greeted by his friends, especially Frau von Stein. He only hoped they would accept his explanation for Anna's presence.

"She's charming, Goethe. For a moment I feared you had taken a new lover," Frau von Stein said mockingly. Goethe had expected no less from her. He was used to her little jabs. So, he did what he usually did and ignored what was said.

"Herr von Goethe just has a tender heart. He cannot resist taking in those in need of his assistance," Herr von Bendeleben said with a wink.

"There, you are right, Bendeleben. I am certain my influence will find her a suitable husband," Goethe gave back. He eyed Bendeleben for a moment; the man was a gentleman and unmarried. Of respectable birth and with an impressive yearly income from his estate. Perhaps—

"That should not be too difficult, I'd say." Bendeleben sipped his tea with a nod at Goethe.

"And why is that, Herr von Bendeleben? Our dear Goethe cannot even find a suitable match for himself."

"Have you come to harass me again about how I lead my life, Frau von Stein? If so, I must disappoint you. I will not discuss this matter with you or anyone."

"The whole city is talking. She is pregnant again! Good grief, Goethe! Marry that poor woman or send her on her way."

"Now, leave him. We have not come here to meddle in such matters," Bendeleben said, waving her off.

"So why have you come then? What is the pleasure of your visit?" Goethe took an expected sip of his tea.

"Your play!" Frau von Stein clapped her hands excitingly. "Everyone at court cannot wait for it. You must put it on. And soon. The duke himself has inquired about it, so I'm told."

"He has indeed. The other day, he asked me about it himself when I was at court for some business." He took another sip of tea to test Frau von Stein's patience—a little revenge for her earlier impertinence seemed only fair. He studied her overly eager face for another moment and then set the cup down as slowly as he could. "It is almost finished," Goethe assured her. She squealed in delight and clapped her hands again. He couldn't say he wasn't pleased about her eagerness. The play was indeed almost done. It had taken him longer than anticipated, but Geist's reaction when he had dictated the first acts had told him this tragedy would be well received.

Goethe went upstairs. Each step groaned under his weight. When he arrived on top of the landing, he looked down the hallway toward Anna's room. He ran his hand through his hair and made his way to her door but stopped short of knocking. Geist had reported to him that he had found Anna in the library in the early morning hours. It struck him as odd, and he was intrigued to find out why she was engaged in reading Greek tragedies.

Reluctantly, he lifted his hand once more but dropped it again almost immediately. He turned around on his heel and made his way to the kitchen. He would ask Christiane to send Anna to the library to meet him there.

Minutes later, Anna appeared at the door of the library. She appeared stoic but was rubbing the scar at the base of her left thumb, which told him she was nervous.

"Come in, dear. How is your hand? I pray it has properly healed?" he asked.

"It is perfectly healed. Thank you," she said and let go of her left hand. "You asked to see me?" She looked at him in anticipation.

"Geist reported that he found you in the library early in the morning the other day." He studied her face and saw the muscles in her face tighten. "Reading Euripides's tragedies," he added. She didn't react but looked down at the floor, so he continued. "I'm rather fond of Euripides myself."

She looked up at him in surprise. "You are?"

He nodded and started pacing. "I've been working on a tragedy myself, inspired by two of Euripides's tragedies." He came to a halt in front of her and looked at her inquisitively. "Which do you favor?"

She looked at him in confusion. Maybe Geist had misread the circumstance in which he had found Anna.

"*Troades*," she said suddenly.

He nodded knowingly and then felt a smile steal across his face. So, Geist had not been mistaken. He cleared his throat. "Why *Troades*?" he asked and started pacing again.

"I've always been fascinated with the Trojan War. My grandfather—"

"Pastor Brion. Of course," Goethe exclaimed. He had educated her; he would have taught her about the ancient Greeks and their wars.

"It's not so much the war that intrigues me," Anna said, interrupting his thoughts. He turned to her in surprise. "It's the suffering of the Trojan women after the war had ended. It's been women's plight throughout history to suffer at the hands of men in conflict, has it not?"

He was astounded at her words but found this the most opportune time to test her. "Was it not three goddesses, Hera, Athena, and Aphrodite who set the wheels of war in motion with their dispute about beauty? It was a man that was able to end the dispute, was it not?"

She chuckled, but then she focused her eyes on him. "A woman was kidnapped and dragged off. Hardly an appropriate reward."

"You forget that it was the goddess Athena who aided the Greeks in their campaign against Troy. Women instigated this war. You must agree," he said, enunciating "women" carefully.

"Immortal women. Fickle goddesses. Not earthly women, always at the mercy of the gods and..." She paused and looked him straight in the face that he felt he had to clear his throat. "And men."

"I must say, you astound me, my dear." He shook his head in disbelief. "I'm sure your grandfather considered, that it is not advantageous for a woman to speak her mind so freely."

"You mistake my grandfather. He encouraged me to speak freely. And to read what I could."

He took a step toward her, but she retreated. Out of fear of him? He wasn't sure. He did not want to cause her any grief, so he attempted a smile. "You may use the library whenever you please, Anna," he said, hoping his softer tone would make her more amicable. "Any book in here is yours to read. Freely."

For a moment she looked pleased, but then her countenance grew dark. "Why did you lie to them about me today?"

Her boldness put him at a loss for words, but he cleared his throat quickly. "To protect you, Anna."

"I think it's rather the case that you wanted to protect yourself. I did not ask to come here."

Her words stung him. "And I did not ask you to come here," he replied.

He saw her wince and draw her lips into a tight line, and he knew he had hurt her. He slowly raised his hand to apologize, but she went to the door. Before she left, she turned around. "'Weep for the fate that has made you captives in this land!'" Then, she walked away.

He stared after her as Euripides's words echoed in his mind. Did Anna consider herself his captive? Had he treated her as such? He swallowed hard and sank onto one of the chairs. How he regretted his words. To his friends and her.

But then he had to smile to himself. While he couldn't reveal that he held her womanly opinions in high regard, he felt a sense of pride that she had shared them so freely with him. He shook his head with a chuckle, then slapped the table with a "ha" and went to his study to work on his tragedy.

Anna was lying flat on her back, staring at the ceiling of her bedroom which had several cracks. But it was almost completely dark in the room, and she could not make out the crevasses despite the shutters to her bedroom window not having been drawn. She had left them open on purpose because she loved how the moonlight fell through the window into her room. It reminded her of Sessenheim. It reminded her of home. She sighed and turned to lie on her left. She had been trying for an hour to fall asleep. Her mind was racing. She was upset at her father, for his words had been very clear. He did not want her there, and he had not acknowledged her as his daughter. Not in front of his friends, at least. Which meant he would not acknowledge her in society, either. It had stung. She had come here to find a suitable match, aided by her father's good name and influence. How was that possible if he denied his parentage? All she wanted now was to go home. But that was impossible. She had promised her mother and her grandfather.

There was a soft knock on her door. Anna hushed her thoughts and stilled her breathing, pretending to be asleep. Who would come to her room at this hour? There was another knock and then the door creaked open. Anna turned around to see Christiane, dressed in a voluminous nightgown filled out with her protruding belly. A nightcap that seemed so little compared to the rest of her body adorned her head. The flickering light of the candle she had brought with her fell onto the wardrobe in Anna's room. The door was ajar, and the beautiful fabric of the dresses that hung next to her country dress glittered in the candlelight.

Christiane hadn't said a word yet, and Anna got up on one of her elbows to look at her expectantly, wondering what had brought her to her bedroom this late. Maybe she needed something. Or was the baby coming? "Is everything alright, Christiane?" Anna was sitting up now, trying to make out Christiane's face in the flickering candlelight.

Christiane came over to her bed and set the candle holder on the night table, right next to the book she had taken from the library. "You're still dressed, my dear?" Christiane looked at her in surprise. "And your shutters are not drawn. Are you trying to escape?" She chuckled.

Anna wanted to feign protest but then reminded herself that Christiane was just teasing her. "I love how the moonlight falls into my room. I hate the dark." She turned toward the window and looked at the almost full moon outside. "I simply don't tolerate complete darkness well. I need some light even if it's just the slightest. And isn't the most reassuring light that of the moon?"

As a child, she had been afraid of the dark and had begged her mother to leave the shutters open. That kind of darkness, where one could not even make out one's hand right in front of one's eyes, was all engulfing and suffocating. She gazed at the moon for a moment, and her mother's lullaby about the rising of the moon came to mind. She had begged her to sing it over and over again until she had drifted off to sleep. Anna hummed it quietly. "Do you know it, this lullaby?"

"Of course, I do." Christiane smiled warmly at her. "Let's leave the shutters open tonight. But you must change your attire." Christiane studied her face in the semi-darkness and then placed her palm on Anna's right cheek. "You haven't said much all afternoon, and you didn't come to supper. Are you unwell?" Anna shook her head and Christiane dropped her hand. "Is everything alright, Anna?"

Anna swallowed hard to keep the tears at bay, but she failed. Against her will, the droplets began to flow. She wasn't sure if Christiane's caring nature, her homesickness, or her father denying her in front of his visitors caused her to weep. She sniffed back the tears.

"You can tell me." Christiane placed her hand on Anna's.

Anna wiped at her tears with the other hand, and Christiane lowered herself down on the bed to sit next to her. Anna wasn't looking at her but straight ahead. She feared Christiane's kind and concerned face would make her break out in tears again.

"He doesn't want me here. And he told his visitors that I'm the daughter of an old friend." Anna knew that if anyone would understand how she felt, it was Christiane. She turned toward her and saw in the flickering light of the candle that Christiane indeed understood.

Christiane patted her hand. "Well, your father cannot hide you from the world like he is hiding me. He knows that I am the only one who will put up with it." Anna smiled faintly at Christiane's words. "You must miss your family dearly," Christiane said softly. "And your father is very happy you're here," Christiane added, trying to reassure her.

Anna swallowed hard but the tears came flowing again. She felt Christiane's arm around her shoulders. "I don't want to be ungrateful. You have been so kind to me." Anna sniffed.

"I don't think you ungrateful." Christiane paused and then nodded to herself. "I know now why your father was so quiet all night..." Christiane turned to her, face beaming. Anna was bewildered by the sudden shift in Christiane's mood. "Until he announced that he would take you to the theater with him next month."

"He said that?" Anna asked with raised eyebrows.

"Yes. Believe it, dear." Christiane looked her square in the face. "It seems he wants to make amends with you." Christiane pushed herself up from the edge of the bed with some effort. She smiled at Anna. "Be patient with him. He has yet to get used to the thought of being the father of a young and handsome woman." Christiane picked up the candle holder and started for the door.

Anna glanced over at the small secretary in the corner of her room next to the window. For a moment, she studied the almost completely spent candle sitting on top. She turned to Christiane. "Would you mind leaving me your candle?"

Christiane smiled. "Of course, my dear." Anna went over to her and took the candle out of Christiane's holder then opened the door for her. "Good night, Anna! Everything is going to be fine; you shall see."

Anna forced a smile and nodded. "Good night!"

Christiane disappeared through the door. Anna closed it quietly behind her and then walked over to the secretary. She pushed Christiane's still burning candle into her holder on top of the tiny stump of candle left in there and unlocked the secretary. With another look at the moon outside her window, she sat down on the chair and then opened a drawer. The wood creaked, and she stopped. Very carefully, she pulled it out further, trying hard not to make any noise doing so. The open drawer revealed sheets of paper, a quill, ink, and a leather-bound notebook. Anna took the notebook and found the last page she had written on. She dipped the quill into the ink, and with another brief gaze at the moon outside her window, began to write.

While much work was waiting for her in the early morning, she yearned to write. When she wrote, she was home. Back in her grandfather's parsonage where she was a daughter and granddaughter. Wanted and needed. Where she had always been acknowledged despite the unacceptable circumstances of her birth.

Chapter 5

1802

Anna stepped outside the house and glanced at the carriage that was waiting for her. The sun was about to set, and Erhart had lit the lamps on her father's coach. Goethe was talking to his old servant but when he spotted her, he broke out into a smile and nodded approvingly. Was that pride she detected in his countenance? Christiane had helped her dress for the theater in a beautiful light blue gown made of satin, chosen for her from the collection of frocks that hung in the wardrobe of her bedroom. Christiane had helped her tighten the corset and had curled her hair into a fashionable updo, finishing it off with a ribbon that circumvented her head. When Anna first saw herself in the mirror, she was astounded. Not as surprised as she was when Christiane disappeared for a moment into her own bedroom on the way down to reemerge with a beautiful silver necklace that she clasped around Anna's neck.

Her father came over to her and led her to the carriage. She didn't meet his eyes. They had hardly spoken in the last two weeks. Erhart was holding the door open, and Goethe held out his hand to help her climb in.

"I am pleased you agreed to come, Anna."

Anna nodded coolly and didn't meet his eyes. On the one hand, she was still cross with him, on the other, she tried to hide her excitement. She took his hand and climbed in. When she was seated in the dark carriage, she saw Goethe give a nod to Erhart before climbing in himself. He sat down across from her, but she could not read his face. It was too dark in the carriage. When the coach jerked forward, she brushed her skirt down and then folded her gloved hands in her lap. She didn't want her father to see how her hands trembled with excitement.

It was a short ride to the theater. After only a few minutes, their carriage pulled up in front of a building that seemed to have been erected only a few years ago. The columns at the main entrance glistened from the lit torches in front.

"We've arrived at the *Komödienhaus*. The duke had it built and made me its director."

Anna raised her eyebrows. "You're the director?"

Her father was the theater's director? The hint of pride in her father's voice hadn't escaped her. It made sense. Her grandfather had asked her to read not only his poetry but his dramas as well. They had left a profound impact on her. His lyrical fervor and profound musings on nature and love, full of passion and longing, had captured her long ago. But while his odes, elegies, and ballads were unmatched, it was his tragedies that had stirred her heart and mind. The characters in his tragedies struggled against societal constraints, a struggle she found all too familiar. Sometimes it was difficult to see that the man she called father now was indeed the poet and playwright Goethe. How she wished she could write like him. She had never spoken to him about his works, and he probably didn't know that she had read all of his dramas. But she couldn't imagine them being performed on stage. They were meant to be read. Was she wrong? She looked at the man across from her and wondered if it was one of his tragedies that would be performed tonight.

Goethe hit his upper thighs with the palms of his two hands. "We should get inside. What do you think?" He smiled broadly at her. Anna nodded and returned the smile. He seemingly was excited. And so was she. Goethe climbed out of the carriage first and held out his hand to help her out.

Outside, she examined the building in front of her more closely. The torches cast light and shadows onto the stairs. While the exterior of the theater was stately, and majestic and gave the appearance of importance, the warm inviting glow from the interior projected an aura of mystery and intrigue. Out of the corner of her eye, Anna noticed her father studying her with an expression of pride. He offered his arm, and she took it, letting him lead her up the stairs and inside the theater.

To her surprise, her father didn't guide her to their seats in a box as he had mentioned on the way but rather backstage where it was cramped and tight and she had to let go of his arm to be able to pass through the narrow hallways, cluttered with all manner of theater business. She had difficulty keeping up with him, and not only for his fast stride. She was fascinated by the hustle and bustle of the backstage, but it seemed all so chaotic. Stage sets and props lined the walls; actors, stage workers, and carpenters were busy getting ready for tonight's performance. When her father passed any of them, they greeted and sometimes bowed to him. Goethe began to hastily point things out to her as they passed them. She eagerly wanted to catch everything he said, but it was impossible as the noise swallowed most of his words. He finally stopped in front of a room in a much quieter area backstage. "This is Demoiselle Schröder's dressing room. Excellent actress." He pointed at one of the doors. "We keep all the costumes over there—"

Men called out to Goethe. He turned to face her. She felt flush with excitement and hoped he wouldn't notice. "Anna, I have to leave you now." He looked around for someone and spotted a young man close by. "You... come over here for a moment!" The young man in his twenties, who had been adjusting some ropes tied around a pillar, looked over his shoulder with a questioning gaze. He let go of the ropes as Goethe motioned for him to come over.

The man strode toward them. "Sir?"

"What is your name again?" Goethe asked him.

"Friedrich, sir."

"Ah, Friedrich. Right. Friedrich, this is Anna. I want you to show her around while I'm getting dressed."

"Getting dressed?" Anna blurted out. She glanced around as if her surroundings offered any answers.

"Yes, sir," Friedrich called after Goethe, who was already hurrying away, calling out to people as he passed them and giving them instructions.

Anna was still staring after her father who had just left her with a stranger and already disappeared into the crowd of backstage workers. She turned and caught Friedrich studying her. "Pleased to meet you. Friedrich, is it?"

Friedrich grinned. "Friedrich it is. The pleasure is all mine, Demoiselle." He bowed slightly. "Now tell me, what do you know about the theater?"

Anna looked around again. "I have never seen anything like this."

"Have you ever seen a play? On stage, I mean."

Anna shook her head. "I have read plays. But I don't know anything about the theater, I'm afraid."

"Well, tonight, Anna, you shall get to know it." He gallantly held out his arm. Anna hesitated for a moment but then slipped her arm through his.

Goethe exited the dressing room as he brushed down the folds of the tunic he was wearing. He felt slightly uncomfortable and exposed in his getup, but the seamstress had done a fine job sewing the attire of a 400 BC Greek nobleman. He was certain he'd give Anna a fright.

He looked around and clapped his hands a few times to get everyone's attention. "Everyone ready in five minutes!" he called, not looking at anyone in particular. People ran past him, and he maneuvered through the chaos to get to the stage.

"Let us congratulate you," a voice called out to him. He turned around and saw Frau von Stein and Herr von Bendeleben come toward him.

"You have not seen it. You should wait and see if I deserve your praise," Goethe said while greeting them.

Frau von Stein mustered him from head to toe. "My dear, Goethe, I must say... you're taking me by surprise with your costume." She unfolded her fan and pretended to hide her face behind it. "You'll make all the women blush."

"A Greek statesman, Goethe?" Bendeleben asked.

"Of sorts. I shall give nothing away," Goethe said. Behind his friends, he saw Anna and Friedrich engaged in conversation, walking toward their group. Friedrich's eyes were wide, talking intensely and gesturing wildly while Anna was staring at him, her mouth open. In shock or awe, he couldn't tell from this distance. Anna and Friedrich appeared so absorbed in their conversation that they had yet to notice him and his friends. Goethe furrowed his eyebrows. What was the boy on about? He would make sure to find out after the performance.

Anna listened intently to everything Friedrich explained eagerly about the theater. She could tell he felt at home here. She was fascinated by his enthusiasm, all the workings of the backstage, and a theater performance he had described to her. She could no longer hold back the question. She needed to know. She wanted to know. "Which play will be performed tonight?"

Friedrich stopped walking and turned to her, head cocked to the side. "You don't know? He brought you here and didn't tell you?" He noticed her confusion and continued. "It's a new tragedy by the great Goethe himself. *Iphigenia in Tauris.*"

Anna shook her head, both in disbelief and awe. Was that the tragedy he had mentioned to her? "Goethe will be acting in it as well. He will play Iphigenia's brother Orestes." Friedrich searched her face. "Did he tell you that he is also the director of our little theater?"

"He did... He did tell me that," Anna said absentmindedly and started walking. Friedrich followed. Out of nowhere, Frau von Stein, Herr von Bendeleben, and her father appeared in front of her. What was her father wearing? She couldn't help but stare. Was that a Greek robe? His legs and arms were completely exposed. The little bit of Roman-like armor he wore over the tunic only covered his loins partially. She tore her eyes away from him.

"Anna!" Frau von Stein stepped toward her, and they both curtsied toward each other. Bendeleben bowed to her, his eyes admiring her gown. "You do remember Demoiselle Anna, Herr von Bendeleben?"

"Of course, I do. How could I forget?" He took her hand with a kind smile and kissed it. "I am pleased to make your acquaintance again, Anna." She nodded briefly and curtsied to him as well. She looked around for Friedrich, but he had disappeared.

Her father cleared his throat, and everyone turned to him. "I must make haste." He took Frau von Stein's gloved hand and kissed it. "Do be generous with your praise after. I beg you." He looked at Anna and back at Frau von Stein. "I arranged for Anna to join you and Bendeleben. Would you mind keeping her company tonight while I'm... otherwise engaged?"

"It will be our pleasure," Bendeleben said and offered his arm to Anna. "Anna?"

Anna avoided looking at her father. She took Bendeleben's arm, and they walked off, following Frau von Stein. Anna glanced over her shoulder, but Friedrich was nowhere to be seen. She swallowed down the disappointment. She had liked the enthusiasm with which he had described the theater and his work as a carpenter who helped build the set. He was about her age, and she liked his natural demeanor. She preferred it over the formality with which her father's friends met her. But Friedrich was gone. He hadn't even taken leave of her. Perhaps some formal etiquette would have been agreeable. She straightened her shoulders and swallowed down any remaining disappointment. She was here to see a play, her first play. Which also happened to be her father's newest tragedy and a Greek one at that. She thought of her notebook and her futile attempts at writing her own. It was all Euripides's fault. But it didn't escape her that her father had found similar inspiration in Euripides's tragedies.

They entered a box that was framed with opulent draperies of brocade. Bendeleben offered her the chair next to his. Frau von Stein sat down behind them. Within moments, Frau von Stein began fanning herself, and Anna couldn't understand why. The theater was rather cool. Involuntarily, she had to think of her father in his scant tunic. She shook her head at the image and looked around. Friedrich had called it a little theater, but she had never seen so many chairs all at once.

"Do you like the theater, Anna?" Bendeleben asked.

"I must admit, I've never had the pleasure before."

"Are there no theaters in Strasbourg?" Bendeleben's brows furrowed. For a moment, she wondered what they would think if they knew she'd grown up in a humble village parsonage instead of Strasbourg as her father had claimed.

"There's none better than our theater here in Weimar, be assured," Frau von Stein said, leaning toward them from behind. "Grant you that we do need to improve its comforts." She suddenly lowered her voice but was still loud enough to be understood. "See the duke and his wife in the box over there?" Anna craned her neck to get a glimpse of them. They looked stoically straight ahead toward the stage. The duke seemed still young, perhaps in his thirties, but his figure belied his age. His wife, the duchess, had a delicate physique, but perhaps she appeared so due to her husband's broad stature. She seemed rather timid despite her station. "He never misses a performance, especially by his minister," Frau von Stein continued. "He adores our dear Goethe. He's the one that convinced him to come and settle in Weimar away from the tedium of practicing law in Frankfurt. Goethe happily obliged, believe me. The court... we've never been the same ever since his arrival, don't you agree, my dear Bendeleben?"

Bendeleben nodded. "True, indeed."

Frau von Stein retreated with a satisfied grunt. Bendeleben leaned over to Anna and whispered. "Now Goethe is trying to convince the duke to build our *Komödienhaus* into a national theater. Wouldn't that be—"

The oil lamps on the walls were dimmed and only now did Anna notice the small torch lights that lit up the stage. The backdrop showed a painted grove of trees with a Greek temple. She wondered if Friedrich had built it. Far off in the background was a deep blue sea. Anna leaned forward. She could feel Bendeleben's eyes on her, but she soon forgot about him and everyone else around her.

A woman appeared on stage, dressed as an ancient Greek priestess. Her body was completely shrouded in white cloth, her head adorned with a wreath of laurels. Anna was utterly engrossed, not only by her beauty and presence but also by her soliloquy. She barely dared to breathe, afraid of missing a single word. Iphigenia, daughter of the Greek King Agamemnon, lamented that she had been condemned to live in exile from Greece among the barbaric and violent Taurians. She longed for her home and homeland. Anna could feel Iphigenia's sting in her own heart. Her eyes filled with tears, and she now wished she had a fan like Frau von Stein to hide behind. She exhaled slowly to compose herself and felt Bendeleben's eyes on her once more. She bit her lip to keep it from trembling and swallowed hard to prevent the tears from falling.

Bendeleben's hand searched for hers, found it, and squeezed it ever so slightly, but she didn't look at him. After a moment, he cleared his throat and let go. Anna focused her eyes on the Greek priestess once more and drank in her words, words she had to remind herself had been written by her father. She shook her head in awe.

At that moment, he stepped onto the stage wearing the same costume she had seen him in backstage. She could hear a few gasps from the audience. Even the duke was leaning forward in his chair, his eyes transfixed on Goethe who dramatically held out an arm toward Iphigenia.

"If social bonds or ties more closely connect thee with this house, as this thy joy evinces, rein thy heart; for insupportable the sudden plunge from happiness to sorrow's gloomy depth. As yet thou only know'st the hero's death."

Anna, too, had her eyes locked on her father who played Orestes, Iphigenia's secret brother. While the actress's playing was captivating, her father's performance appeared rather wooden. Nevertheless, all eyes were trained on him as he revealed his true identity to his sister Iphigenia in the third act. This time it was Frau von Stein behind them who gasped. Anna was rather unsurprised, having read Euripides's play about Iphigenia.

When the play was done, everyone around her got up and clapped enthusiastically. The curtain fell but reopened shortly thereafter with the actors bowing to their audience. Anna caught the proud look on her father's face. Frau von Stein repeatedly called 'Bravo' from behind her, and when Goethe stepped forward and bowed again, the audience erupted in thunderous applause. Anna saw Goethe bow to the duke and duchess, and they proceeded to leave. Even after they had left, people continued to clap. Anna couldn't take her eyes off her father, but Bendeleben offered his arm and led her out of the box and down the stairs toward the entrance hall.

Frau von Stein awaited them there. "I must tell Goethe how splendid it was. I cannot wait. It has been a pleasure, Anna. Bendeleben." Frau von Stein said abruptly. She curtsied to them but didn't give them a chance to reply before she marched off in the direction of backstage.

Bendeleben chuckled and addressed Anna. "I saw that you enjoyed your first play."

"It was wonderful. Such beautiful verses. I wish we would still speak that way." Anna didn't care if he thought her forward. She had no qualms about showing how thrilling she had found it.

"That would be quite entertaining indeed," he tittered.

"It seems you do not take me seriously, Herr von Bendeleben."

"I certainly do, Demoiselle Anna." He bowed to her with a smile, then cleared his throat. "You must join us again sometime."

"I would like that very much. Thank you," Anna said with a genuine smile.

"May I take you home?"

Anna looked at him in surprise. "Oh, no. Thank you. That won't be necessary. I'm supposed to wait for my... Herr Goethe here in the entrance hall."

"Very well. Then at least let me express my gratitude to you for your company this evening." He took her hand and kissed it lightly. "Good night, Demoiselle."

Anna curtsied with a smile. "Good night to you, too, sir." Bendeleben gave a quick bow and left. She followed him with her eyes until he had disappeared through the doors, then looked around her. The vestibule with its beautiful domed ceiling was clearing out, but her father was nowhere to be seen.

"I hope you enjoyed your first visit to the theater and your first play, Anna," she heard someone call out to her.

Anna turned to see Friedrich striding toward her, smiling broadly. She clutched her chest. "You took me by surprise, Friedrich!"

"So, the play. How did you like it?"

"It was splendid indeed. The actors. How they made it come to life. And what beautiful words..." She trailed off with a faraway look, trying to remember some of the verses.

"I take it you enjoyed it, then." Friedrich grinned at her.

"How could I not? This is so much better than just reading them."

"What did you think of Goethe as Orestes?" Friedrich inquired.

"I very much enjoyed Orestes's reunion with his sister. The climax of the play," she said, keenly aware that she had avoided answering Friedrich's question directly. She did not feel like commenting on her father's acting or costume. "I must say that Iphigenia was downright brilliant."

"Very much so," Friedrich agreed. "Corona Schröter is simply captivating."

"Indeed. I believed her struggle," Anna said, deep in thought.

Friedrich raised his eyebrows. "Struggle?"

"Yes, she must grapple with her loyalty to her family and her duty as a priestess." Anna swallowed, realizing why Iphigenia's character meant so much to her. She could relate to her plight.

"Indeed, she does," Friedrich said admiringly, studying her face.

Anna cleared her throat. "Now, you must tell me, did you help build the set?"

"I sure did. Together with three other carpenters," Friedrich said proudly.

"Diana's temple. How beautiful it was. I felt I was in Greece."

"You should let the master know how you liked the play." Anna nodded and searched the entrance hall again. Friedrich must have noticed, for he continued. "The director isn't done yet. He got held up. His coach is waiting for you outside to take you home."

"And he sent you to tell me," Anna concluded.

Friedrich simply shrugged with one of his shoulders and let her lead them to the exit. He walked her down the stairs where below, Goethe's carriage was already waiting. Erhart opened the door for her, ready to help her in, but Friedrich was faster and offered his hand. "I hope you will visit our humble theater again sometime?" he said with a smile.

"I would not pass up an opportunity to see another play, whoever the playwright might be," Anna said and took his hand to climb in. Friedrich nodded with a grin and shut the door behind her. "Good night, Friedrich."

"Good night to you, too." Friedrich stepped back and bowed. He then hit the carriage twice with his open hand, and it jerked forward, driving off into the night with its only passenger. Anna watched the theater disappear into the night through the window. Friedrich was still standing where she had left him, the torches casting fleeting light and shadows onto his face.

Chapter 6

1802

The cold was creeping up her bare feet, so Anna rubbed them together for some warmth. She was wearing only her shift and a blanket around her shoulders. The cold of the night was the only time she could enjoy her father's library unnoticed.

She was sitting at the big oak table at the center of the room, bending over a book. Several other books lay open around her as well as her leather notebook, a jar of ink, and a quill. The only light came from the candle she had carried with her from her room to the library. She avoided using the oil lamp. Erhart would certainly notice if he had to refill it constantly. So, Anna used the candles Christiane gave her. She was surprised that Christiane had not questioned the abundance of candles she had been requesting.

Anna put down the book and rubbed her fingers. Even though it was late summer, it had been a cold, wet season, and the old stone house was always cold at night at any time of the year, Christiane had told her. Anna couldn't agree with her more. She picked up the quill, dipped it into the open jar, and began to write in her notebook.

After a few lines, she leaned back in the chair and stared into the dark library, where the books on the shelves seemed like ghosts, encased in near-total darkness. Anna stood up, took the candle, and walked over to the ghostly shelves, biting her lower lip. The candle brought the books she passed to life, if only for a moment. She stopped and pulled out a book but shook her head. It wasn't the one she was looking for. She put it back on the shelf, continuing her search. After a few rows, she paused again and nodded to herself.

"There you are," she said and was surprised how loud it rang in the silence. She pulled the book quickly and returned to the table. Ignoring the quill and her notebook, she paged through the book until she had found what she was looking for. She read eagerly and didn't even notice the door opening. But it creaked, and she jumped slightly in her seat. Anna held her breath until she saw Christiane appear, carrying a candle herself. The room lit up a little more when she slid in. The look on Christiane's face told her she wasn't pleased to find Anna in the library.

"What are you doing in here in the middle of the night?" Christiane said with concern in her voice, the light from the candle painting her face a menacing mask.

"Reading and some writing," Anna said, shifting uncomfortably on the chair. Only now did she notice how hard it was. Christiane stared back at her in utter disbelief.

"At this hour? I understand you fancy books and like to be in here when your father and Geist are gone, but in the middle of the night?" she asked incredulously.

"You need my help during the day. I won't be reading then. And it's so quiet in the house at this hour."

"But it's freezing in here, Anna. Think of your health." Anna smiled at Christiane's worried face. She knew that Christiane wasn't really cross with her, only concerned. Christiane stepped closer to the table. "What have you been reading?" She made a sweeping gesture with her hand toward the array of books on the table.

"Tragedies... plays. Mostly," Anna said.

"Oh! It was right of your father to take you to the theater, then."

"It certainly was." Anna smiled. "Don't you fancy it? The theater?"

"I certainly do. But I prefer outdoor plays. The theater can be so... suffocating, can it not? I've been saying to your father that we needed to have more plays under the stars outside of Weimar. He was not disinclined."

"Oh, that would be wonderful," Anna said, trying to picture a stage under a group of trees.

"I still prefer a good country ball to sitting still for hours," Christiane added. She looked at Anna's notebook. "May I?" Christiane didn't wait for Anna's permission before picking it up. "What is this?" She leafed through the notebook and then looked at Anna. "You write as well?"

Anna stood up from the chair and tried to find a polite way to seize her notebook back, but Christiane kept turning the pages. Occasionally, she looked up at Anna with narrow eyes. After what seemed like an eternity, Christiane paused, absentmindedly looked for a chair, and sat down, reading eagerly. Turning page after page. Anna nervously bit her lip. No one had ever read her writing before, and it made her incredibly uncomfortable having Christiane read the words that laid open her soul. She began to notice the cold engulfing her, traveling from the soles of her feet all the way to her face, where it met her flushed and hot cheeks. Anna shivered, wondering if it was the forlorn cold or the horror she felt seeing Christiane read her writing. She sat back down, hoping that Christiane would notice her movement and stop reading.

"I'm not a good reader and understand only little of such matters, but your writing..." She looked up at her.

"Yes?" Anna leaned forward. "What about it?"

Christiane stared at her and then shook her head. "It is as I would read your father's verses. How— Child, you must show it to your father at once when he returns." Anna moved closer to Christiane and snatched the notebook from her. Christiane's brows furrowed.

"I shall do no such thing and bother him with my futile attempts," Anna said, pressing the notebook tightly against her chest. She went over to the table and closed all the books she'd been reading.

"But—" Christiane got up.

"I will not allow it," Anna said more forcefully than she had intended to. She had always felt rather silly about her writing. And showing it to a renowned writer, playwright, and poet like her father was out of the question. She would not embarrass herself and expose herself to such ridicule. "Please understand," Anna added more softly. She didn't want to be harsh with Christiane, who had been nothing but kind to her and only meant well.

Christiane placed a hand on Anna's shoulder. "You are truly his daughter. You're a poet like him, Anna. It's obvious."

Anna looked at her in disbelief. Christiane nodded with a smile and left. Anna stared at the closed door and pulled the blanket more tightly around her shoulders. She glanced at her notebook on the table in front of her. And then broke out into a smile. She grabbed the notebook, opened it, and found the page she had been working on. Looking for the quill, she sat back down and started writing again. With each line, her smile broadened, and her confidence returned.

It was a rather chilly, gray morning for late summer when Anna went to the market. She pulled the scarf tighter around her shoulders and fought the wind tearing at her skirts. She was alone today. Christiane was not feeling well this morning, and the doctor that her father had summoned immediately had ordered her to stay off her feet and remain in bed until the day she would deliver their child. It was only a matter of days now.

Although the weather was uncomfortable, Anna was in no haste. She enjoyed time to herself, being out of the house, and getting some much-needed air, even though the air of Weimar was not as fresh as in her village. It rather stank in various places, and if one got a whiff of it, one would not call it refreshing by any means.

Today, Anna didn't mind the plume of smells. She strolled through the stands until she came up to Herr Kurz, who greeted her happily.

"I have everything ready for you, Demoiselle Anna." He came over and took the wicker basket from her.

"You are kind, Herr Kurz. How are your wife and the children?"

"So kind of you to ask. They are fine. Just fine." He carefully placed the fresh produce in the basket and handed it back to her.

"Will you need any help with that?" asked a voice from behind her. Startled, Anna turned around to see Friedrich standing behind her, hands in his pockets and grinning at her startled expression. "I certainly didn't mean to startle you, Miss Anna," he said with a laugh, holding up both hands in defense.

"It seems to me that you purposely tried to do just that, Friedrich," she said with playful exasperation. She nodded her thanks to Herr Kurz and walked past Friedrich.

"May I?" Friedrich pointed at her full basket.

"You may. Thank you." Anna handed the basket over to him and walked on. Friedrich followed her, then came up to her right side once they had left the market square. For a moment, they walked on in silence.

"How have you been?" Friedrich asked, shifting the basket to his right arm.

"Very well. Thank you," Anna said. The air felt like it had warmed up, and she loosened the grip on her scarf.

"I consider it my great fortune to have met you today," Friedrich said suddenly. Anna looked at him, hoping she wasn't blushing as she so easily did. Before she could respond, Friedrich went on. "I wanted to ask you—" He broke off, shifted the basket to his left hand, and stopped walking. Anna followed suit. His face was unreadable as he continued. "I wanted to ask you... I... May I call on you sometime?"

Anna broke out in a smile, which Friedrich returned, seemingly relieved. How handsome he was when he smiled, the fine lines around his green eyes framing them like ripples on a pond. They reminded her of the gentle ripples that disturbed the surface of the pond near her grandfather's parsonage. Anna studied his face for a moment and then thought it was best to give Friedrich, who gazed at her with bated breath, an answer. She cocked her head.

"I dare say you may, Friedrich," she teased and started walking. Friedrich hastened after her. "I have not seen much of Weimar or its surroundings, you know. Maybe you could show me?"

"It'd be my pleasure." Friedrich bowed slightly to her, grinning.

For the rest of the way back to her father's house, Anna asked Friedrich a stream of questions about the theater. Friedrich happily answered them all. When they arrived at the house, he handed her the basket and bowed to her to take his leave. She watched him for a while as he walked off. When he was almost out of sight, he suddenly turned around, tipped his hat to her with a smile, and started whistling a tune. Anna laughed and rewarded him with a wave of her hand. She turned around to open the door, fully aware that the smile on her face seemed rather too big.

Anna and Christiane's maidservant rushed around in the kitchen. Both had their sleeves rolled up to their elbows and wore their aprons. Together, they lifted the cauldron in which they had brought water to a boil off the stove. Anna sighed in relief when they had finally managed to set it down. She took a neatly folded stack of linens and draped it over her arm, then jumped slightly when a piercing scream echoed through the house. The servant placed a hand on Anna's other arm. Her eyes were worried, but her smile attempted to be reassuring. It was more of a grimace. "The mistress has done this several times. She knows what to do."

Anna gave a nod back, but the servant's words had not stilled her worry.

With a ladle, the servant began scooping water from the cauldron into a waiting bowl. Once it was filled, she picked it up, ready to leave the kitchen. Anna wanted to follow her with the linens, but the door burst open, and a distraught and disheveled Goethe stormed in, almost running into the servant with the bowl of hot water. He was only dressed in breeches and an unbuttoned shirt, surprising considering the cold autumn day it was. He glowered at Anna and the servant as if they were to blame for what was happening to Christiane. Anna motioned to the servant to leave, and they both slid past him out of the kitchen.

Christiane's eyes were closed, and her breathing was shallow. Too shallow, Anna thought. It came as no surprise. Christiane was very weak after the whole ordeal; that much was clear. She looked rather small and forlorn in her bed. No belly was protruding from underneath the shift Anna which the servant had helped her into after washing her body. She was still perspiring, so strands of hair stuck to her forehead. Anna took a cloth, wet it, and sat down beside Christiane to wipe her face.

The doctor at the foot of the bed rolled down his sleeves, dipped his hands into a bowl of water, then cleaned his instruments in the same way before wiping them dry and placing them back in his bag. He walked over to a nearby chair to pick up his waistcoat, but to Anna's surprise, he didn't put it on. Instead, he came over to her and put a hand on her shoulder. Anna stopped wiping Christiane's face to turn around and look up at him.

"All she needs is rest now. You have been of great help. I'm not sure she would have made it without you at her side," he said and then cleared his throat. "She will need your company in the next few weeks." The doctor took his hand off her shoulder, nodded goodbye, and left the room.

Anna turned back to Christiane and searched her face. Her usual rosy cheeks were a pasty white. She seemed to be in a deep sleep now. Good, Anna thought, sleep would numb the pain. With a sigh, she stood up, but Christiane opened her eyes at the same moment. Her hand was searching for Anna's. She sat back down and gently stroked Christiane's hand. "You need to rest now."

Tears rolled down Christiane's face. "God punishes us, Anna! Another child stillborn. How can that be?" She sniffed, turning her head to the side and toward the window. "God punishes us because we share a bed without the blessing of the church."

Anna thought of her mother but had no words of comfort for Christiane. She just kept stroking her hand, hoping it would distract her from the pain in her heart. After a moment, Anna noticed that Christiane had drifted off to sleep again. She carefully let go of her hand and pulled the blanket over her more tightly before tiptoeing out of the room. After she had closed the door quietly behind herself, she leaned against it. She was utterly spent but tried to muster any ounce of energy she had left to fight the resentment toward her father she felt rising up within her.

She heard voices below and walked to the staircase to peer down. Below, near the front door, the doctor was taking his leave from her father. The older man put his hand on her father's shoulder as he had done with her. Goethe looked entirely distraught. His eyes were nailed to the floor and his hands balled into fists.

"There's nothing I could do for the child. I'm sorry," the doctor said with a pitiful look at Goethe, who neither met his eyes nor responded. The doctor eyed him carefully but then his hand sank to his side. "I will let myself out." With that, the doctor opened the front door and disappeared through it into the dark outside.

Goethe looked up, dazed as if surprised, and stared at the door. He put his hand up against it, let it rest there for a moment, and then slowly shut it. He turned around and with the back of his head leaned against the now closed door. He slowly slid down until he sat on the floor, knees bent and with his back leaning against the painted wood. He buried his head in his hands and started sobbing, silently. Anna drew back quickly and folded an arm against her belly. Any resentment she had harbored against him for his refusal to commit to marriage had completely evaporated. She felt only pity now. He had lost just as much as Christiane. For the first time, she understood that he loved Christiane and the life they had created together. Only the devil knew why he hadn't married her yet, but he was as much a husband to her as any man who had shared his marriage vows at God's altar. Anna swallowed down the shame she felt and promised herself to never allow herself to think less of him or Christiane again.

Their spoons clinked against the porcelain. But not everyone present was eating. At the head of the dinner table, Goethe was simply staring down at the plate of soup in front of him. August and Anna, who sat across from each other, spooned the hot liquid in quietude.

Anna looked up and turned her eyes from father to son and back, unsure if she could interrupt their thoughts or the silence that hung in the room like the heavy air before a thunderstorm.

The maidservant came in and out of the dining room, bringing different dishes from the kitchen, which she had tried to keep warm over the stove. Each time she entered, Anna was glad to see her, but the maid remained engulfed in silence, refusing to utter a word. Her gaze was lowered, her lips drawn into a tight line. She moved through the room with great care, as if not to disturb the leaden silence.

Anna noticed that August finished his soup at almost the exact same time as she did. They glanced at the other and then together at their father. Goethe sat as still as a statue, staring into his untouched soup as if it held the answers to unspoken questions. It appeared as if he deemed himself utterly alone in the room, not once acknowledging their presence.

Anna studied her father's demeanor nervously and then cleared her throat as loudly as a lady was permitted.

"Will you not try my cooking?" she asked into the silence. August stared at her with wide eyes, which then flitted back and forth between her and Goethe, who didn't react at all to her question. Had he heard her? She gave a slight start when her father suddenly flicked his eyes to hers, like a ghost in a painting that one wouldn't expect to move. His eyes appeared as if he had been called back from a faraway place.

"My cooking. Will you not try it?" she asked again, noticing that the palms of her hands had begun to sweat. August shifted uncomfortably in his seat.

"I feel no need to eat tonight. If you will excuse me..." With that, Goethe left the dining room in a trance. All they could do was stare at the door that closed behind him.

"The last time it happened... he was like that for weeks," August said, his voice hollow.

"Weeks?" Anna couldn't fathom bearing this silence for another day, let alone weeks.

"And then he left and was gone for months," August added.

"But your mother... she needs him now." Anna could feel her face darken.

August lowered his eyes and opened his mouth as if to speak but closed it again with a shake of his head.

The kitchen was the warmest room in the house. Anna was making tea while Christiane sat on the chair next to the warm stove, a thickly knit shawl draped around her shoulders and a glass of red wine in her hand. She was still weak, but the color had returned to her cheeks. After a couple of weeks in bed, Christiane had decided that she could no longer bear to be confined to her room and bed. Anna was unable to convince her to stay in bed as the doctor had ordered. She on being up, but Anna and the maidservant refused to let her do any of the cooking yet.

"He's leaving tomorrow," Christiane said, looking over the rim of her glass at Anna.

"August mentioned to me that he might." Anna shook her head and felt her hand tighten around the handle of the teapot.

"I cannot blame him." Christiane took another sip of the blood-red liquid. She burped involuntarily and her hand flew to her lips. "I apologize," she said.

Anna walked over to Christiane, took the wine glass, and placed a cup of tea in her hand instead. "I think you should blame him. He ought to take care of you and be at your side."

"He's grieving, Anna."

"So are you."

Christiane lowered her eyes at Anna's words and stared at the cup in her hand. "Maybe... Maybe now is the time to talk to him again," Anna continued. Christiane waved her hand dismissively. "About marriage I mean."

Anna wasn't sure if it was terror she saw swimming in Christiane's eyes, or defeat. "I could not."

"But you believe your children are stillborn because God punishes you. Because they are born out of wedlock. You said so yourself." Anna felt guilty speaking so plainly to Christiane. She was only trying to convince Christiane to speak to Goethe. To tell him what she wanted. And needed.

"What do you believe, Anna?" Christiane asked, interrupting her thoughts. "Is God punishing us?"

"May I be frank?" Anna asked.

Christiane waved her hand to proceed. "Of course." And with a quick laugh, she added, "You have been nothing but frank, my dear."

Anna gave a soft laugh, but her expression soon turned serious. "I believe my father ought to have married you a long time ago. And you should talk to him again. Before he leaves."

"It's not my place to approach him about such matters." She got up and put the still full teacup on the table.

"You bore him three children. You have shared his bed for years. Isn't that enough reason?"

Christiane sighed and leaned against the table. "I could not. He wouldn't want it." Her words seemed final.

"You go rest. I will finish cleaning up here," Anna said, her voice heavy with defeat. Christiane only nodded. Her face looked drawn. She grabbed the wine glass, and before she disappeared through the kitchen door, she turned around, steadying herself against the door frame with her other hand. "I'm not the only one who cannot muster the courage to talk to him," she said. "I still think you need to show him your writing."

Anna knew she'd been caught in her own hypocrisy. How could she tell Christiane to be brave when she feared the same? She straightened and gave Christiane a firm look. "That would not be wise. And especially right now. If even my cooking doesn't please him, how could my writing?"

"He cares more for you than you think," Christiane said, eyeing the bottle of wine on the table. "As much as every child I bore him." She walked over to the table, grabbed the bottle, and made her way out of the kitchen. "No tea for me today, Anna," she said over her shoulder as the door swung shut behind her.

Chapter 7

1803

There was a loud rap on the front door. Anna could hear it all the way from the library where she was pouring over her manuscript. It was Erhart's duty to mind any comings and goings, so she dismissed the interruption, dipped her quill in the ink jar, and began writing again.

She jumped when there was another knock, this time louder. She furrowed her brows at the sight of the ink stain running into the last word she had written and sighed in frustration. Where was Erhart? Anna pushed back the chair and made her way to the front door.

There was no sight of Erhart anywhere. Anna peeked through the narrow window next to the tall wooden door and shrunk back in surprise. She quickly looked back over her shoulder, but the hallway behind her lay quiet.

Anna suppressed the smile she noticed forming on her lips and opened the door. Outside stood Friedrich, his hat in hand, greeting her with a broad grin, clearly relieved it was she who had opened the door. "Good day, Anna!"

"Friedrich! What are you doing here?" Her question immediately erased the smile on his face, and she regretted her briskness. But in fairness, she had not seen him in months. "Do you wish to speak with Herr Goethe?" she asked. "He still hasn't returned."

"I have not come to speak with him," Friedrich said with some confusion. "You agreed I could call on you. When we spoke at the market," Friedrich said, his eyes fixed on her as if to will her to remember. She remembered, but after a few weeks had passed, Anna concluded that he had not meant to call on her after all. "Well... are you coming then? The weather is perfect, and the day is not getting any younger. You do want to explore Weimar, don't you? You said so."

In all her time in Weimar, no one had taken her around the city or surrounding areas. Anna knew the parts of the city where she had been sent to do errands or accompany Christiane or her father, but nothing beyond that.

"I do. But I thought you— Today? Now?" Anna was completely caught by surprise. Not only did Friedrich's call come rather unexpectedly, but she had been completely immersed in her work and ached to return to it. "I don't know." She hesitated. "I'm needed here. I can't just leave."

"Won't you ask him in?" Anna turned around in surprise and saw Christiane standing by the staircase, watching Friedrich with unabashed curiosity.

"Pleased to meet you, Madame," Friedrich said, bowing to Christiane.

"Your friend is charming, Anna. Now, don't let him just stand there. Ask him to come in at once," Christiane said, urging her with a look. Anna relented, stepping aside and motioning for him to come in. She almost wished her father was here. He wouldn't have been so welcoming to Friedrich.

"What is your name?" Christiane asked, taking a step forward. Anna looked around for Erhart, who was still nowhere to be seen.

"Friedrich Lorenz, Madame." Friedrich stood a bit forlorn in the hallway with his back toward the front door.

"And what is the occasion of your visit, Friedrich?" Christiane was relentless.

"I'm here to take Anna for a walk and show her—"

"I cannot afford to leave. I'm sorry. Not today," Anna cut him off.

Christiane stepped toward them. "Why not, Anna? It's a lovely day. Just perfect for a walk."

Anna tried to make Christiane understand that she didn't want to go, but Christiane either ignored or didn't understand her pleading eyes.

"I cannot just leave you."

"Nonsense! Go on. I'll be just fine." Christiane dismissed them with a flick of her hand.

Anna looked from Friedrich to the sunlight that shone through the small row of windows to the left and right of the front door. She remembered the warm spring breeze that had brushed her face when she had opened the door. It was the perfect day to explore Weimar. Maybe her writing could wait. She longed for a bit of fresh air and sunlight after spending much of the winter months indoors. She could continue writing tonight.

Christiane walked over to the hooks on the wall behind the staircase where an array of coats and shawls hung. She grabbed a shawl and walked over to Anna. "It's settled then." She held the shawl out to Anna who took it and wrapped it slowly around her shoulders, mumbling a quiet thank you. It was hard to ignore the twinkle in Christiane's eyes.

"I'll be back before dinner," Anna said, not looking at her.

"Not necessary. I feel like cooking today."

"But—"

Christiane held up her hand to stop her. "The servant will be there to help me. Don't you worry about me, Anna. Just be back by dusk." She took Anna by the shoulders, turned her around, and gave her a subtle push toward the door where Friedrich was still rooted in the same place.

"Give me a moment, Friedrich." Anna remembered that her books, notebook, and writing lay open on the library's table. Only Christiane knew about her writing. If August or Erhart found it... The thought made her shudder. She walked swiftly to the library, collected her things, and brought them upstairs to her room. By the time she arrived in the foyer again, she had to catch her breath.

Without a word, Friedrich opened the door for them, and Anna stepped outside. She had to shield her eyes from the bright sunlight. When she was down the steps, she turned back around. Christiane gave her an encouraging nod and waved goodbye. Friedrich put on his hat and tipped it toward Christiane, taking his leave. He then leaped down the stairs and hurried toward Anna. His broad smile made her lips curl up in return. There was a lightness about him that instantaneously dispersed any melancholy that might have made her heart heavy. They started walking and Friedrich began pointing out buildings and landmarks to her. Although Anna knew the streets and sights around her father's house very well, she just listened, letting the smooth tenor of his voice make her fall into step.

Hours later, Anna's back ached and her feet were on fire from the long way they had come. She wasn't used to walking this much, especially not in the fine shoes that Christiane had ordered from the shoemaker for her. The leather was soft, but the shoes were certainly not ready or fit for a rigorous and prolonged walk such as this. They had left the city of Weimar behind them at least an hour ago and were strolling on a small path outside of town toward a village, between fields of stunning yellow that rivaled the bright sunshine.

"What is this flowering plant? I've never seen it around Sessenheim," Anna said, motioning to the yellow plants around them.

"Woad," Friedrich explained. He went to the edge of the field and pulled one out to hand it to Anna. "It used to grow all across the duchy, but these are one of the last fields left. You make blue dye with it."

"A yellow plant becomes blue dye?" Anna stared at the fields around her incredulously. How fascinating. Friedrich had told her that he had not enjoyed much schooling and had entered an apprenticeship to become a carpenter when he was fourteen. But to her great surprise, he had a wealth of knowledge. She had asked him how he had become so learned and had found out that he loved books just as much as she did. It had been a pleasant surprise, as much as their walk today. She had enjoyed Friedrich's company and stories as they explored every corner of the city, but it was beyond the city walls that she truly began to feel at ease. How she missed Sessenheim. She couldn't help but sigh.

Friedrich noticed her change in mood. "I hope today has pleased you."

"Very much so. I'm much obliged, Friedrich." She looked at him carefully. "If only my feet didn't hurt so much," she said with a painful expression on her face.

Friedrich laughed heartily. "I have brought you far. We shall take a rest." He looked around and spotted a small stream with a makeshift bridge close by. To Anna's surprise, he took her hand and led her to the water.

She pulled off her shoes with a groan, sat down on the grassy bank, and let her feet fall into the water. A moan escaped her throat. "This feels so nice," she said, closing her eyes and leaning back in the grass. While a bit too cold for her taste, the water immediately stilled the fire burning up her soles and toes. Friedrich scooped up some water and splashed his face. He then dipped a kerchief into the water to press it against the back of his neck. He, too, moaned in relief. They remained in silence for a few minutes, enjoying the stillness of the moment. The buzzing coming from the grass and fields around her, and the soft gurgle of the stream threatened to lull Anna into sleep. She quickly sat up, picked up her shoes by their laces, and stood.

"Are you refreshed?" Friedrich asked, squinting at her through one eye.

"Yes, thank you. My feet are much better." She let her eyes wander across the surrounding landscape. "It's lovely out here." She started walking, swinging her shoes in her right hand.

"Won't you put your shoes back on?" Friedrich asked, staring after her in bewilderment. He got up and scampered after her.

"I walked barefoot outside all the time back home," she said over her shoulder. She saw the bridge before her and grinned. Once on the bridge, she turned around and blocked the passage across. "Til here and no farther!" Anna called with outstretched arms. Friedrich slowed his step, his lips twitching with amusement. "I believe we have left the town. Where are you taking me, sir? We shall go no farther until you've told me."

"I wanted to take you to this spot right here, Demoiselle. These are the gardens of Weimar." Friedrich was making a sweeping motion with both of his arms. Anna giggled, glad to see Friedrich took her tease in stride and played along. "How could I not show you the true beauty of this town?"

Anna let her eyes wander around in a dramatic and exaggerated fashion. "And who tends these gardens, sir?" she asked, trying to stifle a chuckle.

"Those who seek them." Friedrich removed his hat and bowed to her.

"You're quite the poet," Anna remarked.

"Only in your presence," Friedrich said, walking onto the bridge. Anna laughed softly. He stepped closer to her and looked into her eyes. "Do you wish to return to the city?" His voice was husky.

Anna closed her eyes for a moment and sighed audibly. She could feel the heat of Friedrich's body close by. Clearing her throat, she opened her eyes and stepped around Friedrich to lean against the bridge's railing. "No. Not yet. It feels like home here." She closed her eyes again and let the sounds of nature and the light breeze that smelled of freshly cut grass wash over her.

She noticed Friedrich coming up beside her and opened her eyes to look across the fields. Friedrich followed her gaze. His hand was resting next to hers on the railing. "Do you miss where you come from, Anna?"

She turned toward him. His friendly, ever-so-green eyes kindly studied her face. "Yes, but especially my family. My mother... she is ill. She needs me, but she wanted me to come here. And my grandfather. He taught me everything I know."

"What about your father?" He looked at her but then shook his head to himself. "You must excuse my forwardness," Friedrich said ruefully.

Only now did Anna notice Friedrich's hand on hers. She carefully pulled out from underneath; her face suddenly hardened. He had no right to inquire about her father. And she could hardly tell Friedrich about him. What would he say if he heard that Goethe himself was her father? How would he treat her then? Would his hand still have rested on hers? She could still feel the warmth. Without a word, she sat down and pulled on her shoes.

Friedrich looked puzzled. "My apologies. You must think me impertinent," Friedrich said. Anna stepped around him once again and walked off the bridge toward the city. Friedrich followed.

"It will be dark soon," Anna said over the shoulder.

Friedrich walked up beside her and fell into step, his face concerned. They strolled in silence, the city's buildings drawing closer and the failing sun dipping the fields around them into an orange glow.

Just as night was falling, Goethe's house came into view as they entered the square dominated by its imposing presence. She was glad they had made it in time so she wouldn't worry Christiane unnecessarily. She glanced at Friedrich by her side. They had barely spoken a word on their way back. She swallowed, regretting her reaction to his question.

The city had fallen quiet and the lights from houses they passed began to illuminate the cobblestones. Anna saw that Erhart had also lit all the lamps in her father's quiet house. Again, Anna wondered where he had been this morning. She dismissed the thought and fastened her eyes on the front door. She would have to bid Friedrich a good night soon and felt a pang of sadness at the thought. Surprised by the feeling, she shook her head. Friedrich noticed and looked at her. His face was unreadable. She attempted a smile, and he returned it.

Suddenly, a carriage came rushing around the corner and toward them. Dust and debris flew. Friedrich jumped out of the way and pulled Anna with him. She found herself wrapped in Friedrich's arms, feeling the tensed muscles underneath his shirt. He was breathing heavily, nostrils flaring, and shaking his fist at the carriage that had come to a halt in front of her father's house. A man's head peered out of the window—it was Herr von Bendeleben, examining them with furrowed brows. Friedrich released Anna and marched toward the coach as Bendeleben stepped out.

Ignoring Friedrich, Bendeleben walked past him toward Anna and bowed. "Anna, I'm surprised to see you out at this hour."

Anna curtsied. "I'm just returning home from a walk." She motioned to Friedrich. "Friedrich here was so kind to show me around Weimar since I had not yet seen all its splendor."

"It would be my pleasure to show you around sometime in a more, should I say, comfortable way, and at a more appropriate hour," he said with an arrogant side glance at Friedrich.

"Thank you but I—"

"Is Herr Goethe home, Anna?" Bendeleben asked briskly, cutting her off with a look at the house.

Anna was taken aback at his abruptness. "He's not. He has not yet returned from his travels." She studied Bendeleben's face in the semi-darkness. "Is everything alright, Herr von Bendeleben?" Anna asked softly. The lines in Bendeleben's face were more marked than usual, even in the waning light.

Bendeleben turned to her and seemed surprised she was studying his face. "I see. Do you know when he is to return?" he asked, his tone growing gentler. Anna simply shook her head. She knew from Christiane that it could still be weeks before her father would return. Bendeleben suddenly bowed. "I'm sorry to have disturbed you, Anna." He bowed again and then went to climb back into his carriage, pretending Friedrich did not exist. Friedrich stood rooted in the same place, his face darker than the drawing night. When the coach drove away, Bendeleben stared determinedly straight ahead without a glance at her.

Anna shook her head in confusion and hurried toward Friedrich. She needed to get inside quickly before Christiane started worrying. Together they walked to the door, and Friedrich knocked loudly.

For a moment, both stood in silence, but then Friedrich suddenly turned to her.

"A true gentleman, isn't he?" Friedrich looked over his shoulder in the direction in which the carriage had disappeared. "I think an apology for almost running us over would have been appropriate."

The door creaked open to reveal Erhart, more disheveled than usual.

"I had a wonderful time. Thank you, Friedrich," Anna said without looking at him but at the tips of her shoes that bore the dust and dirt of the day. Christiane would not be pleased. "Weimar is not so bad after all," she added with a tiny smile she hoped Friedrich would notice.

"It was my pleasure. Good night, Anna." Out of the corner of her eye, she saw Friedrich take off his hat and bow slightly to her.

"Good night, Friedrich." With that, Anna slipped into the house. She put her hands on the wooden door and indicated to Erhart that she would close it. He shuffled away. She watched as Friedrich returned his hat to his head and walked down the stairs. With his back to her, he paused for a moment to look into the sky. She could hear him sigh. He then strode across the square. Anna watched him until his shape disappeared around a corner.

Chapter 8

1803

Anna sat across from August at the table in the library. He was holding a book and reading while Anna leaned back in her chair, arms folded.

"Do you know what the best part is?" August asked, putting down the book. Anna shook her head, smiling. "I'm really learning it this way," he added.

"I'm glad to see you finally enjoy reading Greek," Anna said with a laugh.

August joined in the laughter but then grew somber. "It's because you're here. Studying Greek with me."

Anna smiled at him. She knew he loved to have company in his studies. The tutors were rather strict and demanding, and Goethe had high expectations for his son. She unfolded her arms and leaned forward. "Should we continue then?" she asked with a smile and wink.

"As you wish." August exhaled loudly, followed by a huff. "You never seem to grow tired of it."

"No, I don't. So, let's do some more declensions," Anna said with a laugh, leaning back in her chair again.

August sighed heavily. "Alright then. *Philia*!"

"Feminine. First declension." She closed her eyes. "*Philia, philias, philiai, philian*!" She opened her eyes. "Correct?"

Just as August opened his mouth to answer her, the door swung open, and Christiane appeared. "Your father has returned!" she said breathlessly, her face beaming with excitement.

Christiane was gone as fast as she had appeared. Anna and August both stared at the door. Then, their eyes met.

"Already?" August asked with raised eyebrows.

"Already? It is well about time if you ask me. But yes, I'm glad he wasn't gone as long as you had predicted," Anna said and stood up.

"It will be good for Mother." August followed suit.

"Not for me, however. If your father is back, that means Geist is back as well," Anna said, her eyes narrowing and lips pursing.

"That is not so bad, Anna. As for me, I'm desperate for a break from Greek," August said with a grin and proceeded to gather up his books. He tucked them under his arm and left the library, leaving the door open for Anna to follow.

"I am glad to see that you have been keeping up with your studies, young Master August," Anna heard Geist say just outside the door. She sighed. She was in no mood to see or speak to Geist. But she had no choice, so reluctantly, she followed August out of the room. Geist wouldn't be happy to see her exiting the library, but that might be as well.

Geist was right outside, greeting her with a half-arrogant, half-angry glance. "Neglecting your duties once again?"

Anna straightened her shoulders. "And what do you think these duties are that you presume I'm neglecting, Herr Geist?" Anna asked, unclenching her jaw. She didn't want Geist to get the better of her.

"The duties that ensure that you have food on the table and a roof over your head," Geist said with a smirk.

"That's enough, Geist." Goethe appeared beside them, carrying packages under both arms. Christiane and August were right behind him. August peered angrily at Geist along with Goethe. "It seems to me that you are the only one here neglecting your duties, Geist." Her father's voice was stern and cold. Geist looked flabbergasted and embarrassed, like a child who had been caught in mischief. He bowed slightly toward Goethe and, ignoring the others, proceeded in the direction of the study.

"If he does not improve his manners, I will have to send him on his way," Goethe said, his voice kinder now. Anna managed an unsure smile. "Now, these are for you all," Goethe motioned with his chin to the packages clamped beneath his arms. He thrust a package at August. "For you, my son," he said cheerfully. Anna couldn't remember a time she'd ever seen her father so happy.

"Thank you, Father," August said, his voice husky with excitement. Anna chuckled at August's innocent display of eagerness, eyeing the wrapped item he was holding now in both hands.

Then Goethe handed a package to Anna. "This is for you, Anna."

Anna looked at him in surprise. Christine smiled at her and nodded in encouragement with a hint of satisfaction. Anna thanked him, quietly, and took the large box from his hands.

Goethe handed the last package to Christiane. "This is for you, my dear."

"You're too kind, Herr Goethe." She smiled broadly at him. "We are happy to have you back."

"Now tell me. Will it be long 'til supper? One of your hearty stews would be most welcome tonight." He winked at her.

"Then you have come to the right house, Herr von Goethe," she answered with a laugh and an eager nod as she headed toward the kitchen.

Anna had carried the big package to her room and was now sitting on her bed, staring at it with a mixture of anticipation and dread. With a weary sigh, she untied the rough hemp string and peeled the paper away, already knowing its contents. It was the type and size of the box that had given it away. As she lifted the lid and pushed aside the delicate tissue paper, beautiful muslin fabric embroidered with gold stared back at her. She ran her fingers across and admired the fine material. With a swift movement, Anna pulled the gown out of the box. For a moment, the white muslin with the gold embroidery reminded her of Iphigenia and ancient Greece. It was a stunning gown indeed. In her mind, this was possibly the most beautiful gown she'd ever possess. It wouldn't do for court, but that's why she liked it. It was light and airy and not heavy like the brocaded silk gowns the ladies in high society preferred to wear, some of which hung in her wardrobe. She admired it for a moment longer but then walked over to her wardrobe to hang it up next to the other beautiful gowns she had been given since arriving in Weimar. Many of them were made from the finest silks but impractical and opulent. She could hardly wear them around the house where she preferred to wear her country dress. The gowns in her wardrobe were more appropriate to wear to the theater. While she loved the gown her father had brought for her, deep down she wished he had brought her books.

There was a knock on the door. "Come in," Anna said while she closed the armoire.

August stuck his head in. "Supper is ready."

"I'm not hungry really," she said and sat down at her desk.

August came inside and quietly shut the door. "But Father is home. He would like us all to eat with him." He walked over to her. "What is it, Anna?"

"I'm just not very hungry tonight, that's all. I do not want to upset him by just sitting there and not eating. He seems so cheerful and without worry."

"He won't be happy if you will not eat with us." He took Anna's hand and pulled her up. She let him. "Come on. I have not seen Mother smiling so for weeks."

"There you're right." She ruffled his hair, and he pushed her hand away with a laugh. "You go ahead. I will be right down. I just have to clean this up." She pointed at the paper and box on her bed.

"What did he bring back for you?" August asked, eyeing the pile of tissue paper on her bed.

"Another gown," she sighed. August nodded knowingly. "It is beautiful. Very beautiful," she added. She didn't want to appear ungrateful. "What did he bring you?"

"What do you think? Books, of course," August said, not making any attempts to disguise his disappointment.

"Poor August," Anna said with a grin and shoved August toward the door. She ignored the sting she felt, grabbed the pile of paper and the carton, and followed August out of the room. "Well, let's not let your father wait. He seemed rather ravenous for your mother's stew."

A few days later, Christiane came to Anna's room in the afternoon. Anna was hunched over her desk when Christiane came in. She had knocked but had not waited for Anna's answer. Anna looked up in surprise.

"Your father would like to see you in the parlor," Christiane said, looking expectantly at her.

"He would?" Anna had fully turned around now, watching Christiane go toward her wardrobe.

"You must put on the dress he got you."

Anna raised her eyebrows. "Why? To see him in the parlor? This gown is rather—"

"Yes," was all Christiane said as she opened the doors of the armoire and pulled out the muslin gown. She admired it for a moment and then turned to Anna. "Let me help you get changed."

Her eyes wandered to Anna's hair and her eyes narrowed. "And fix your hair."

Anna stood and held up her hand to stop Christiane, who was already trying to pull off her apron. "What's all this fuss? What for?"

"You have a visitor, and your father wants you to look presentable," Christiane said while carefully spreading out the gown on the bed. "I will help you get changed."

"Who is it? It must be Frau von Stein herself if he wants me to wear this gown," Anna said wryly.

Christiane frowned. "Not quite, dear." She had already proceeded to undo Anna's laces. In no time, she had Anna in only her shift in front of her. "Oblige your father, would you?" Christiane tightened Anna's corset and pulled the muslin gown over her head.

"Why aren't you telling me, Christiane? Who has come to call?"

"You will see. Patience, my dear." The older woman pulled her over to the chair and sat her down, the skirts billowing around Anna. Christiane went to work and set her hair. Everything was done in a hurry, but Christiane pulled Anna off the chair and shoved her in front of the mirror. "Beautiful. Just beautiful!" She exclaimed, clapping her hands. Then she pulled Anna's face close and pinched her cheeks.

"Ouch! What are you doing?" Anna tried to wipe Christiane's hands away.

"You need some color in your cheeks, my dear. You've been sitting in your room writing all hours of the day. You look positively pale!" Christiane shook her head. "Your writing will cost you your health, you know," she said sternly. Before Anna could respond, Christiane pulled her out of the room and down the stairs.

Christiane knocked on the parlor's door and went straight in. Anna followed her reluctantly. She was curious to see who had come but also felt a sense of apprehension. She felt awkward and overdressed for the occasion in the gown her father had gifted her, but at least she did feel beautiful.

Inside the parlor, her father and Herr von Bendeleben stood immediately as Anna entered. Bendeleben was dressed in a fine suit and nervously cleared his throat, clearly admiring her from head to toe. He bowed to her, ignoring Christiane completely. Anna acknowledged him with the slightest, perhaps even angry curtsy at his dismissal of the one who had done her up so beautifully.

Christiane appeared not to have noticed the impertinence of Goethe's guest and beamed from ear to ear, knowing she had pleased Goethe immensely. Goethe dismissed her with a grateful nod. She looked again at Anna and smiled encouragingly before taking her leave. Anna stared after her as the door closed, then turned around to face the men.

"I hope you forgive me for my intrusion," Bendeleben said and bowed to her again.

Anna looked to her father, but his face was unreadable. "Why don't we all sit down and have tea together this fine afternoon? Please, Anna. Come. Sit." Her father pointed to an empty chair at the table. Anna eyed the chaise longue, which was the farthest away, but she followed her father's request and sat down on the chair he held out for her.

Her curiosity got the better of her, so she asked: "What brings you here, Herr von Bendeleben?"

"I wanted to speak with you," Bendeleben said.

Anna raised her brows and looked at her father in surprise. He only smiled encouragingly. What were her father and Bendeleben up to?

"Would you care for some tea?" Anna asked and rose to her feet. Both men stood in surprise as Anna started for the door.

"Christiane will bring us the tea. She'll be here shortly," her father said, motioning for her to sit back down.

"I will go and help her," Anna said quickly and left, hoping her father would not hold her back again. She heard Bendeleben call out a hasty 'thank you' to her before she closed the door behind herself.

She quickly went to the kitchen where Christiane was already preparing the tea. Christiane looked up in surprise when Anna entered.

"What are you doing here, dear?" Christiane asked, wide-eyed.

"What does he want, Christiane?"

"Who do you mean?" Christiane asked innocently.

"You know who," Anna tried to keep the rising anger at bay.

Christiane was arranging the tea pot and cups as well as slices of cake on a tray which she picked up after she was done and headed for the door. "Shall we?"

"I'm not going anywhere if you're not telling me what's going on here," Anna said, folding her arms in defiance.

"My dear. You're as stubborn as your father." She shook her head but then smiled at Anna. "You have caught the man's eye, don't you see?"

"But what does he want with me?"

"It's rather simple, dear. He wishes to speak with you." She looked at the tray. "And have tea and cake. Why don't you just oblige him, hmm?" Christiane leaned against the door, and it swung open. Anna followed her reluctantly.

Anna opened the door to the parlor so Christiane could carry in the tray. To her surprise, her father was no longer there. Only Bendeleben was present. He rose immediately, and Christiane set down the tray. Anna pleaded with her silently not to leave her, but Christiane excused herself.

Anna went over to the tray and managed a smile at Bendeleben. She felt terribly awkward around the man, especially now that she was alone in the parlor with him. It was as if all her movements had become wooden. She poured the tea, commanding her hands to stop trembling. She set the cup of tea and a plate with a slice of cake in front of him.

"Thank you, Anna," he said.

Anna sat down. "What did you want to speak to me about?"

Bendeleben seemed taken aback by her bluntness. He cleared his throat. "Won't you have any tea and cake yourself?"

"Thank you, but I prefer coffee," Anna said. She didn't appreciate the delay in his answering her question.

"Shall we call for coffee then?" he asked with an expectant look at the door.

"That's not necessary," Anna said trying not to sound too unfriendly.

Bendeleben cleared his throat again and lightly coughed in his fist. "Well... I... I wished to ask you if you would allow me to call on you."

Anna stiffened her posture. "Herr von Bendeleben... I will have to speak with—"

"I have spoken with Herr von Goethe. He has no objections," Bendeleben said. So, *this* was her father's scheme. Bendeleben looked at her intently. "I know how much you loved the theater. Let me take you there again. It would be my honor."

Anna perked up. The theater! Oh, how she longed to go back. But then she remembered Friedrich. What would he think of her when he saw her dressed like this with a gentleman like Herr von Bendeleben? "I don't know." She swallowed. "Please forgive me if I have caused you to believe—" Anna stood again and Bendeleben followed suit.

"In no way, be assured, Anna." He stepped closer to her "Please! Let me take you to the theater," he said softly. He reached for her hand and took it up to his lips. Anna stiffened. "I would be most obliged." He kissed her hand and looked deeply into her eyes, and Anna knew it was futile to refuse the man.

After Bendeleben had left, Anna took the tray back to the kitchen where she found Christiane. "How could you leave me alone with him?"

"He wished to speak with you. It was only proper that I left," Christiane said with a low, firm voice.

"It would have been more proper to not be alone with a gentleman," Anna mumbled.

Christiane took the tray from her. "You were in your father's parlor. He is your father's friend and a man of honor."

"Bendeleben does not know that he is my father," Anna reminded her.

"That does not matter now. He's a well-to-do gentleman, Anna. You should consider whatever he wanted to speak with you about."

"He wants to take me to the theater," Anna said.

"Well... isn't that lovely?" Christiane smiled approvingly. Anna didn't want to share her concerns about Friedrich with her. She mumbled a swift goodbye and left the kitchen, eager to be free of the stifling gown.

Chapter 9

1803

Anna glanced at Christiane across from her as the carriage rattled along the dusty country road. Her face was flushed with excitement. It was harvest season, and the smell of hay and the dying sun seeped in through the windows. Anna inhaled deeply. It smelled like home.

Occasionally, they were jerked to their left or right side. Night was beginning to fall, but it didn't convince their driver to slow down. Christiane stuck her head out the window, unafraid to ruin her hairdo. She drew back in and clapped her hands excitingly. "We are almost there."

A few moments later, their carriage reduced speed, and the shapes of small houses passed by them outside the window. Then the coach came to a sudden halt. Anna heard music and laughter, drawing nearer and becoming louder. The driver helped them out of the carriage, and Anna found herself near the market square of a village.

She craned her neck to see where the music came from and saw some villagers assembled for a dance in the middle of the square. Not far off stood tables laden with food, and a large bonfire was burning at the other side of the square. It was a harvest festival like the ones they had in Sessenheim. Anna ignored the sting and let Christiane pull her with her toward the merriment.

To Anna's surprise, they were met by Christiane's maidservant. Other people came to greet them. All of them seemed rather familiar with Christiane who led Anna to a wooden table on which several jugs of wine stood. Without hesitation, Christiane poured Anna a cup of wine, but Anna just shook her head. Wine gave her grave headaches. Christiane knew as much. She only shrugged and put the cup to her own lips, drinking greedily. "It's so good to leave the city and be out here, is it not?" Christiane said between gulps. "Your father won't be gone long but long enough that we can have some entertainment." Christiane winked conspiratorially at Anna, who had to laugh at Christiane's lightheartedness.

"What if he finds out we came here?" Anna asked, eyebrows drawn together.

"Oh, he knows, my dear. I come out here often. Here, I don't need to be hidden from people. They are my kin," Christiane said with a hint of resentment. She poured herself more wine. Even if Goethe knew of Christiane's escapades, Anna wasn't sure if he would approve of her accompanying Christiane.

"Has he ever come here with you?" Anna asked.

Christiane laughed heartily. The wine was taking effect. "Oh no, dear. He does not share my love for dancing. And he does not care too much for the company of the villagers. He's a man of the court, you know." Christiane raised her cup to the sky and cheered the night. "But I hear he has not always been that way," Christiane said wistfully.

"Perhaps that's the man my mother knew," Anna said. She let her eyes wander across the square and the houses lining it. "Indeed this village reminds me of home. We had dances such as this in Sessenheim."

"Then you must be a good dancer!" Christiane exclaimed and put down her cup.

"I never really had the chance to dance much," Anna said quietly.

Christiane lifted one eyebrow in surprise. "Why?"

"I was not a very desirable dance partner."

Christiane's eyes narrowed and she stepped closer, whispering. "But you are very handsome and—" Christiane stopped herself and nodded knowingly. She placed a hand on Anna's cheek. "I know it was not easy for you... growing up without your father. And people punishing you for *his* lapse in... in judgment."

"It does not matter. I never really cared for dancing. As you know, I rather enjoy a good book."

"Indeed, you do, dear," Christiane said, eyeing Anna thoughtfully. But then she clapped her hands. "But tonight, you shall dance, Anna. No one here knows where you come from." Christiane pointed at a group of young men on the other side of the square. She turned to Anna and took her by the shoulder, smiling broadly. "Those young men over there do not seem to care. All they see is a handsome girl in need of a dance partner."

Anna followed the direction in which Christiane was pointing. A young man from the group came striding toward them. Anna swallowed. "See. Tonight you will not lack a dance partner. Be assured."

The young man reached them and bowed slightly to both women. He wore his Sunday best, but his hair was tousled, and a smudge of dirt grazed the side of his chin. "Miss, would you give me the honor of this dance?"

Anna looked at Christiane who nodded encouragingly. "I must warn you, I am not very skilled," Anna said.

The man smiled. "Then I shall teach you." Anna returned his smile and extended her hand. He took it and wrapped it around his arm.

"I'm Anna," she said to him.

"Heinrich. It's my pleasure, Anna." He patted her hand. "Shall we?"

Anna glanced at Christiane, who clapped her hands in satisfaction. Maybe this night would not turn out as bad as she had feared. She saw Christiane whirl back around toward the wine jug. A man around Goethe's age approached her and she immediately turned her attention to him. He bowed to her, and she laughingly took his hand and let him lead her in the same direction Heinrich led Anna. Christiane and the man lined up next to them. Heinrich patiently guided Anna along, and she hoped that he and no one else would notice her inexperience.

The men and women had lined up opposite each other, waiting for the next dance to begin. Anna wiped at her neck with the back of her hand and slightly threw her head back to catch the cool air. She stood across from Heinrich, with Christiane next to her. Anna's face was flushed and her cheeks hurt from laughter and smiling all night. She had danced for almost an hour already but didn't want to stop. The steps were easy for her now, and she no longer needed Heinrich's help. She smiled confidently at him, and he winked at her. He was a handsome fellow, tall and strong with broad shoulders like many young men in the village. During one of the dances, he had to lift her up every so often and had done so with such ease, as if she were light as a feather. He had told her proudly that he was the son of the village's blacksmith.

She turned and found Christiane watching her. She giggled and winked at Anna with a face and nose that shone pink with too much wine. Anna noticed that Christiane's hair had started to come loose. One more dance, Anna thought, and then they needed to get back.

The musicians began to play the next song. Anna looked back at Heinrich, but he had vanished. In his stead stood Friedrich, who bowed to her with a smile. Anna's mouth fell open and she shook her head in confusion. But before she could say anything, the dance began. The dance steps led them closer, and Anna tried to speak to Friedrich but there wasn't enough time. They had to circle around each other and their neighbor first. When Anna danced around Christiane, she mouthed something to her, but Anna didn't catch what she was saying. Then the dance picked up in speed. When Anna finally faced Friedrich and they had to join hands, she hissed: "What are you doing here?"

"What do you think? Dancing, of course."

His answer frustrated Anna, but they had to dance away from each other again and she could no longer question him about his intentions. She looked around for Heinrich but could not find him. The dance was dizzying and everything around her had turned blurry. The tempo finally slowed, and Anna was able to get her bearings. She faced Friedrich once more but looked past him for Heinrich. Her eyes finally found him not far off. He didn't look very pleased. For a moment, she wondered how Friedrich had convinced him to step aside and give up his dance with her.

She looked back at Friedrich when he took her hands in his. "I wasn't aware that you enjoyed dancing," he said.

"I did not. Heinrich over there taught me and now I find it rather agreeable," she said between breaths. Friedrich's eyes grew dark. Was he jealous? "Do you come here often?" she asked him.

"No. Not really. Herr von Goethe employs my mother's cousin. She informed me that you would be here." On cue with the music, he swung Anna around.

Christiane's maidservant was Friedrich's relation? "So, you're following me now?" Anna asked when she had both feet back on the ground.

Friedrich did not answer but pulled her out of the dance and away to a quieter side of the square. She wanted to protest but was too out of breath to get a word out. While she didn't know much about dancing, she knew that one never pulled out of a dance, unless it was for fainting or other emergencies. Every dance followed a strictly set pattern. Their absence from the dance would throw off those who remained. Anna looked over her shoulder at the dancers. Chaos had already ensued.

Friedrich came to a halt and turned to face her. He took her by both of her arms and grew somber. Anna searched his face, confused and wanting to speak, but he spoke first. "Anna! Since I first met you at the theater, I have not been the same," he said, trying to catch his breath.

Anna stared at him with wide eyes. He smiled at her. What she saw in his eyes made her flush and her heart race. His lips parted, but Christiane suddenly appeared next to them. She offered Friedrich a quick but indifferent smile then turned to Anna as if Friedrich did not exist. "It is time... to leave, my... dear," she slurred. The driver. He's waiting."

Friedrich did not disguise his disappointment. Anna smiled at him encouragingly, but he only managed to return a sad frown.

"I'm sorry, Friedrich. I have to go." Christiane was already taking Anna by the arm, to lead her away but also to steady herself. "Good night. And thank you for the dance," Anna added before they started for the carriage waiting to take them home.

When they reached the coach, Anna looked back and saw Friedrich still standing where they had left him. He slowly raised his hand in goodbye. Anna turned back around and helped Christiane into the carriage. As they drove off, Anna peeked out the window to see if Friedrich was still there, but he was gone.

"How could you take her there?" Goethe was tired from his travels and not pleased at the news Erhart had shared with him.

"Anna needs to get out once in a while. She is young! Too young to be tied to the house like this," Christiane gave back from the bed.

Goethe was seated on the chest and pulled off his shoes angrily. "But not to a village dance. It's not proper for her. I'm gone and you—"

"You've never cared that I go," Christiane said, her voice as cold as the floor.

"In her position, Anna should attend a proper dance and not some village... I forbid you to take her again." Goethe shivered as he took off his breeches. He climbed into bed and sought Christiane's body to warm himself, but she withdrew and turned her back on him. He inched closer and put his arm around her. She pretended to be asleep. Goethe sighed and let go of her. He opened his mouth to wish her goodnight but decided against it. He turned to the other side and blew out the candle. His body was exhausted from spending the day traveling on bumpy country roads, but his mind was restless, racing. Anna was beautiful. Just like her mother. Her inexperience made her easy prey. He needed to make sure she didn't meet the same fate as her mother, even if he had been the culprit. Ensuring she'd marry well was his *mea culpa*.

Anna gazed into the brown liquid in her cup. Since coming to her father's house, she had taken a liking to the beverage. Both tea and coffee had rarely been offered at her grandfather's parsonage, simply for the fact that they were rather unaffordable for a village pastor.

She looked at the two men seated with her around the table. Both her father and Herr von Bendeleben preferred tea. Her father had been surprised when Bendeleben had insisted on coffee for her. So was she.

Bendeleben called every week. If her father was home, he joined them. She dreaded Bendeleben's visits when he wasn't. She did enjoy their conversations; he was well-read, and they discussed history and philosophy. He respectfully let her share her opinions but more often than not, he either dismissed them or greeted them with insincerity. If her father was present, it was as if she didn't exist. The two men would fall into deep conversation about politics, history, or any court-related business. She would listen for a while but would eventually lose interest.

"I have not thanked you for the pleasure of your company today, Demoiselle. You must forgive me," Bendeleben said, startling Anna back to their presence and out of her thoughts. Anna smiled but avoided a response by taking a sip from her cup. Bendeleben turned to her father. "You have been traveling rather often lately. For the duke, I presume?" He took a sip of his tea and looked at Goethe over the rim of his cup.

"I have indeed," her father said with a sigh. Bendeleben nodded in acknowledgment. "I can hardly find the time to take care of things at the theater anymore. I will have to bring some more actors to Weimar, so I at least will be freed from having to take on parts myself."

Anna perked up at the talk of theater. Bendeleben seemed to have noticed and smiled at her, then turned to Goethe. "Anna has agreed to accompany me to the theater again."

Her father looked at her carefully, his expression hard to read. "Then you must take her this week, Bendeleben. Schiller's *Maria Stuart* will only run for another few days. It is a superb play."

Bendeleben looked expectantly at Anna. "What do you think, Anna?"

Anna glanced at her father, whose eyes were urging her on. She had no choice but to accept. "You are very kind, Herr von Bendeleben. It would be my pleasure to accompany you." Her father clapped his hands once and let out a satisfied grunt. Anna stared into the little bit of brown liquid left in her cup. It bore a grimaced version of her reflection.

Herr von Bendeleben offered Anna his arm. She took it and let him lead her from the theater into the crowded entrance hall, where those who had attended talked excitedly about the performance. Anna felt flush with excitement herself. Schiller's play had been marvelous. It wasn't just the actors' skillful performances that had captivated her, but the poetic and rather strong words by the female characters. She had been particularly mesmerized when the leading lady delivered her soliloquy with a trembling voice before her execution. If she could only write like that.

"A wonderful play, was it not, Herr von Bendeleben?" Her breath caught in her throat. She tipped her head back and closed her eyes to picture the stage again.

Bendeleben laughed at her enthusiasm. "Certainly. It was well done. You're absolutely right. And what excellent actors." He smiled proudly. "I'm happy you enjoyed it."

"Which of the ladies struck you the most, Elizabeth I or Mary Stuart?" Anna asked him.

He looked at her in surprise but then nodded thoughtfully at her question. "An excellent question indeed," he said. The lines on his face became more prominent as he sank deep into thought. "I must say... Elizabeth I. A most brilliant ruler who understood the demands of the court and did not tolerate any insubordination. Her long and successful rule is evidence of that."

"Indeed." Anna glanced at him with narrowed eyes.

"What about you, Demoiselle? You must surely agree with me."

Anna's eyebrows raised. "I do not, sir." He seemed taken aback, so she continued quickly. "I find Mary Stewart a rather intelligent figure. A paragon of strength and dignity. But a tragic figure nevertheless, unjustly persecuted, a victim of circumstance."

"Unjustly? A victim?" Bendeleben asked, his brows drawing together in confusion.

"Indeed. Was she not destined for and in line to inherit the throne?"

"She was a scandalous whore and murderess," Bendeleben said, his lips drawn into a tight line.

Anna had to swallow her shock. Bendeleben must have seen it because he immediately apologized. "You must excuse my... misplaced use of vocabulary. Please forgive my outburst," he said and bowed slightly to her.

Reluctantly, she nodded as a sign that she accepted his apology, but deep down, she had found his words abhorrent. She straightened her shoulders. "It appears Herr Schiller viewed her just as I did. His play bears her name, not that of Elizabeth I., and it appears she's his heroine, is she not?"

"She is indeed. Again, please accept my apologies. It appears you understand plays much better than I ever could. You and the playwright are of the same mind."

She hated how he had given up so easily and let her win this argument to appease her. Her grandfather would have never given up so readily. Neither would her father, she suddenly realized. She remembered their discussion about the Faust tragedy he had been working on, and how that moment had felt as if she was back in the Sessenheim parsonage debating with her grandfather.

Bendeleben offered his arm. As they walked through the vestibule, people greeted him, but most ignored Anna. It did not seem to bother Bendeleben.

Anna looked around to see if Friedrich was in the crowd. She hadn't seen him before the performance either. Maybe she was in luck and would be able to avoid him. She did not want him to see her with Bendeleben.

However, when they reached the exit, Friedrich was standing by the door as if he had been waiting for her. He stared at them, disappointment swimming in his eyes. She silently pleaded with him and mouthed for understanding, but Friedrich turned abruptly around, and Anna lost sight of him. Before they exited through the door, Anna cast her eyes around once more in hopes of spotting Friedrich, but he was truly gone. Disappointed, she followed Bendeleben to his carriage, which waited below the stairs of the theater. She let Bendeleben help her inside. After talking to his driver, he climbed in as well and sat down across from her.

They drove on in silence for a few moments, the only noise the rattling of the coach and the clatter of horse hooves on cobblestone. She felt Bendeleben's eyes on her while she looked out the window into the dark.

"Everything alright, Anna? You have fallen silent since we left the theater," he asked quietly and carefully. "Are you alright?"

"Yes, of course. I'm fine. Thank you," she said quickly, trying to recover.

He smiled, seemingly satisfied with her answer. "I thank you for the pleasure of accompanying me to the theater. And for enlightening me. You're most... most agreeable. And I apologize for not being so myself."

Anna held up her hands. "Oh no. I must apologize for sharing my opinion so freely. My grandfather— I must thank you for taking me, Herr von Bendeleben."

"Richard."

Anna was puzzled.

"Please call me by my first name, Richard," Bendeleben said with the most charming smile.

"Oh, I see," Anna sputtered.

"And there's no need to thank me. The pleasure was all mine." He cleared his throat. "There is no other I would have liked to take. You make a most agreeable companion, Anna." Bendeleben gazed deeply into her eyes. She blushed, broke his gaze, and noticed that

she was stroking the gloved thumb pad of her left hand which rested
in her lap.

Chapter 10

1804

Goethe looked at Bendeleben across from him with studied concentration. His friend had just presented him with a most agreeable proposal. Although Goethe had been expecting this visit from his friend, he had also dreaded it. His eyes scanned the parlor for anything that might help him with the task ahead. He had withheld matters of great importance from his friend. Bendeleben's expression grew concerned at Goethe's silence. Finally, Goethe sighed. "I haven't been honest with you, my dear friend. You may want to reconsider your proposal."

Bendeleben stood and began pacing around the room, then came to a stop in front of Goethe and raised his arm in determination. "I meant what I said. Now, will you explain your hesitation?"

Goethe stood and started pacing as well. Bendeleben followed him with his eyes in utter confusion. "Anna's father... He is not who you think he is."

"He is a poor man?"

"Poor in judgment, if you will." Goethe faced Bendeleben and straightened his shoulders. He breathed out heavily. "Anna is my daughter."

Bendeleben stared at him for a moment, shook his head, and then broke out into a smile. He went over to Goethe and patted him on the back. "My dear Goethe! That explains her disposition towards books and the theater," he said with a laugh and sat back down. But then he shot up from his seat again and looked at Goethe with determination. "I stand by what I said. I fancy Anna— Your daughter. I want to make her my wife. Will you give me her hand in marriage?"

"You have no hesitations? She is an illegitimate child. I cannot let a mistake of my youth ruin your reputation or standing at court."

Bendeleben stepped close to Goethe. "Old friend, your daughter will be a wonderful companion and an excellent wife. She will make me very happy." Bendeleben stretched his hand out to Goethe. "Do you accept my proposal then?"

Goethe hesitated for a moment. He had wanted no better match for Anna. He was pleased with his friend's proposal and even more pleased with his reaction to his revelation. He smiled at Bendeleben, took his hand, and shook it heartily.

The sun shone brightly onto Anna's writing desk, drying the ink so quickly that she didn't have to use the blotting paper. She was careful that the ink on her fingers didn't transfer to the clean paper in front of her. She wrinkled her nose at her handwriting, which had gotten perpetually worse over time. She blamed her stiff fingers on endless nights of writing.

Someone knocked on her door. She got up, adjusting the shawl around her shoulders, and opened it absentmindedly. Outside stood Christiane, beaming from ear to ear, and holding up a letter. "A letter for you. It was just delivered."

Anna cocked one eyebrow at Christiane's exuberant demeanor and took the letter. "Is it from my mother?" Anna turned the letter to see if it was indeed from her mother, but it wasn't. She walked over to her desk, not letting her eyes wander away from the handwriting, and sat down. Christiane followed her in. When Anna broke the seal, Christiane was by her side, looking on silently. Anna unfolded the paper and began to read. A gasp from Christiane told her she had been reading along. Her hand flew to her mouth as if to smother the gasp while Anna let the letter sink down onto her desk and stared ahead. She shook her head as if to disperse the swirling thoughts, but it was no use. She collapsed against the back of the chair, biting her lip.

"What a fine letter and what a fine proposal." Christiane clapped in her hands. "He is an esteemed gentleman. Very well-to-do. A fine family, too. What a match! Your father!" She started for the door but with a look at Anna, stopped short. "What is the matter, Anna? You should be overjoyed."

Anna slowly turned to stare at Christiane. "I... I don't know what to say. It is so sudden. And too soon."

"Sudden? Too soon? This man has fancied you from the minute he laid eyes on you," Christiane said incredulously, resting both her fisted hands on her hips.

"But I'm of lower birth with no fortune, nor father, as far as he knows. How can he possibly consider me? He has no information about my family or where I come from." Anna shook her head.

"He does not seem too concerned about that, now does he?" She came over to Anna and put her hand on her shoulder. "Count your blessings, dear. You've made a wonderful match indeed. Your father will be delighted."

Anna's eyes narrowed and she stood abruptly. "He wants me to make a good match, doesn't he?"

Christiane looked at her blankly, but then her brows furrowed. "Of course, he does. And I thought it was what you wanted as well. Why you came to Weimar."

"I do not love the man." Anna folded her arms and hoped Christiane would understand.

"Oh, my dear. Look at me." Christiane laughed bitterly. "Love alone does not get you a husband."

Anna fell back onto the chair, defeated. "You're right, he would make a fine husband. I could hardly make a more perfect match, indeed," she said and swallowed hard.

Christiane kissed the top of Anna's head and then placed a hand on her cheek. "You are very fortunate, Anna," Christiane said gently. She patted her shoulder once more and left. Anna stared at the letter in front of her. Her life's course was fated to be determined by men and by the choices and decisions made by men. She felt her throat tighten.

Goethe sat behind his desk and stared at the clutter in front of him. Books, papers, quills, a newspaper, letters. The manuscript of the tragedy he had been working on for over two decades now caught his eye, hovering at the edge of his desk. *Faust*. His magnum opus. Would he ever find the time and will to finish it?

He had much work to do, but he had sent Geist away. He lacked focus today. There was too much on his mind. Bendeleben, Friederike, Anna. He needed to write to Anna's mother. It was long overdue. He sighed, grabbed some paper, dipped his quill in the ink, and began to write. There was no use in delaying the letter to her any longer. He had barely finished the first line when a knock on the door interrupted him. His forehead creased. Everyone in the household knew that when the door to his study was shut, interruptions were not welcome unless it was a matter of urgency.

He stood with a huff and went to the door to open it. "Anna!" He was surprised to see that she was the one who had knocked. She had never sought him out before. Her face was flushed, her long, blond braids hanging over her shoulders. She hadn't worn her hair in that fashion since he had picked her up in Strasbourg. She brushed down her skirt and asked to speak with him without meeting his eyes. He nodded and stepped aside to let her in.

When he closed the door, he wondered why she had come. Something seemed to weigh on her.

"Please, sit down," he said, but Anna only shook her head, her braids dancing on her shoulders, which made her appear younger than she was. He felt his body tense but sat down in his chair behind his desk. "Very well." He looked at her, expecting her to speak, but she did not. Instead, she looked around the room with inquisitiveness, and then her eyes fell on his manuscript. She cocked her head and he saw she was intrigued. He quickly covered it with the stationary. For a moment, Goethe silently urged her on, but he wasn't the most patient man. He cleared his throat. "Now, what did you want to speak to me about?"

Anna looked back at him. There was a quick flash of confusion in her eyes as if she had forgotten why she had come, but then she grew determined. "Herr von Bendeleben. Your friend. He has proposed."

So Bendeleben had asked her already. The man did not waste any time. *Good*, Goethe thought. He broke out in a broad smile. No need to hide that he was immensely pleased. But he froze when he saw Anna's fierce glower. He shifted uncomfortably in his chair. He needed to know where she stood. "Well, will you accept?"

"That is the wrong question to ask," Anna said. Her face was hard, and it was impossible to read her thoughts on the matter. "The question of far more interest is how a man, a gentleman like Herr von Bendeleben, would consider someone like me. He knows nothing of me, my family, or my upbringing."

"You're a handsome girl," Goethe said. Anna only scoffed. Goethe chose to ignore her impertinence and continued. "And you are a proper and educated young lady with very fine manners. All the attributes a gentleman seeks in his future wife." Goethe crossed his arms, pleased with himself.

"But I hardly had the proper upbringing, as you know." Now it was Anna who crossed her arms. "Or the proper family or ties a gentleman like him customarily seeks," Anna added.

"Your father is quite a respectable man, my dear," Goethe quipped and suppressed a chuckle.

"But he does not know who my father is," Anna said coldly.

Goethe leaned back in his chair and eyed her carefully. "He does. I told him."

Anna simply stared at him, flabbergasted. "But then... why would he consider marrying the bastard child of a poet?"

"You know, I'm much more than a poet, my dear. Apart from that, a poet is considered quite a reputable person by most people. Perhaps even admired?" Goethe said with a laugh.

"Not where I come from," Anna said coolly. Both were silent for a moment, but then Anna turned and stepped close to his desk to face him fully. She straightened her shoulders. "How can you expect me to marry someone I do not love if you do not even consider marrying the one that you do love, Herr von Goethe?" She turned around and walked out of his study.

It took Goethe a few moments to recover. He shook his head to get over the shock that she had caught him in his own hypocrisy. But it was not her place to speak to him like this. He had just praised her fine manners. Bendeleben! She had not given him an answer. Would his friend be happy with a wife who spoke her mind so freely? Would he be able to tame that spirited woman?

His eyes fell on the stationary that covered his manuscript of *Faust*. He thought of Anna, her long blond braid, and involuntarily his mind drifted to Sessenheim, to Friederike, who had worn her hair the same way. And Gretchen! Faust! His mind raced. He swiped the stationary away and pulled the manuscript toward himself. Hastily, he searched for the very last page. "The Eternal Feminine draws us upward," he whispered to himself. He took up his quill and repeated the words while writing them down. He had never before understood his inspiration for Gretchen, the young innocent, and pious woman Faust loved, seduced, and ruined with the help of Mephistopheles, but in the end who saved him not only from that devil but also from himself. The realization struck him with such force that his hand trembled. The quill slid from his fingers and left a stain on the page. It was of no concern to him. Tomorrow, he would make Geist rewrite the page.

Anna leaned the back of her head against the now closed door of her father's study. She closed her eyes for a moment and took a deep breath. She had spoken out of place and wondered what the repercussions for her impertinence would be. Surely, there would be. She had seen the shock written all over his face at her words and the way she spoke them. She opened her eyes and with a deep breath, she walked toward the main house entrance, grabbing a woolen shawl off one of the hooks on her way. When she got to the large door, she opened it quietly and slipped out.

A stiff breeze blew. The streets seemed deserted in the dreadfully cold winter weather. Anna pulled her shawl tighter around her shoulders and walked up the stairs to the theater. She gazed up at the tall doors and then at the handle before carefully pushing it down. But the door seemed locked. She pushed harder, even leaning against the door, but it didn't budge. It was locked indeed. She scanned her surroundings. The square in front of the theater lay quiet. Only one man with his head down rushed across the square with his shoulders raised and his collar up against the wind. She looked at the door again and took a step back. The disappointment seeped deeper than the cold wind.

With a sigh, she turned around and slowly walked down the stairs. At the bottom of the stairs, she stopped. Over the howling of the wind, she could hear faint hammering. She tried to listen more intently, but the wind carried off any sound as soon as it reached her ear.

Anna looked around, but not a soul was in sight. She walked around the side of the building through a narrow alley to reach the back of the building. It was completely windstill between the buildings, so she heard the hammering clearly now. It grew louder with every step she took.

When Anna reached the back entrance, she slipped through a back gate where a door stood slightly ajar. To the side of the door was a man pounding nails into slats of wood piled around him, and shavings covered and blew about the ground around his feet. When he turned to pick up a piece of wood, Anna saw that it was Friedrich. He looked up and spotted her but didn't utter a word, instead just staring at her in silence. She wanted to greet him, but he turned away and back to work, hammering louder and more forceful than before.

For a moment, she stood there watching him. Then she straightened her shoulders and walked in his direction. She needed to speak with Friedrich and wouldn't let him deter her from it. Anna drew nearer but he kept ignoring her as if she didn't exist. She walked around him to where she could face him better. To her relief, he finally put the hammer down.

He kept his hands busy and spoke. "You should not be here." He still didn't meet her eyes.

"I need to speak with you," Anna said without trying to hide the urgency in her voice, but Friedrich still didn't react. Had he heard her? Could he not tell that her coming here and wanting to speak with him meant that it was important? Did he no longer care about her? "Please, Friedrich. I must explain."

"No explanation is needed. I understand perfectly," he said, his voice as cold as the wind that tore at their clothes and tousled their hair.

"No, you do not." Anna was getting angry at his stubbornness.

"You appear to seek only proper associations," he said.

Anna noticed the sharpness with which he had said the words. "It is my father that seeks them, not me."

"You do not live with your father. How could he—"

"I *do* live with my father," Anna interrupted quietly.

He turned around toward her. After a moment of confusion, she could see how the truth dawned on him. He put down a tool he had held in his hand, crossed his arms, and studied her face. "You mean... Johann Wolfgang von Goethe is your father?"

Anna looked down at her hands and then back at Friedrich. "He is indeed. He was a student in Strasbourg when he explored the countryside and met my mother. They fell in love, but one day, he left never to return. My mother never told him that she was with child. She awaited a proposal any day. So did her parents, but it never came." Anna swallowed and took a deep breath to continue her story. "Not until last year did my mother tell him about me. She sent him a letter to ask him to take me in. She hopes, away from home and everyone who knows my... situation, I will be able to make a good match with the help of my father's influence." Anna waited for a response, but he was silent. He seemed deep in thought. Anna stepped even closer. "Please, Friedrich. It was not my intention to hurt you." She swallowed. "Please forgive me for not being open with you," she added quietly, lowering her eyes again to watch the shavings dance around their feet in the cold wind.

"And Bendeleben?" Friedrich asked suddenly.

"He has proposed." Anna noticed Friedrich's face fall and he stepped away from Anna, but she saw the anguish in his eyes before he could fully turn away from her.

With his back turned, he said coldly: "Then I do not know why you've come here."

"I need your help, Friedrich," Anna said, stepping closer to him yet again. Friedrich didn't respond, so she hesitantly placed her hand on his back. "I do not wish to marry Herr von Bendeleben. I want to return home to my mother, but I need your assistance to leave Weimar."

Friedrich swung around, and Anna dropped her hand. "You want to leave?" His face was pained.

"I must. I cannot stay here. Not a day longer," Anna said, kneading her hands.

"I will help you. But only under one condition," Friedrich said.

Anna took a step back. "I hope you are not about to make an improper proposal."

Friedrich chuckled and stepped closer to her. "Not at all. My apologies if it appeared that way." He dusted off his hands on his trousers and then took her hands in his. "Will you write to me?" He searched her eyes.

Anna smiled in relief. "Nothing would give me more pleasure. I love to write, in any case."

"You do? I mean, you write?"

Anna pulled her hands free and walked away from Friedrich. With her back turned to him, she said: "Yes. I do. Poetry, but plays in particular. That seems to be the one thing I inherited from my father."

"Will you share your writing with me sometime?"

Anna smiled and turned around to Friedrich. "Someday, I might indeed."

Friedrich walked toward her. "Will we meet again, Anna?"

"*That* you will have to promise *me*," she said with as much sincerity as she could muster.

The candle offered barely enough light to pack. It didn't help that it flickered dangerously in the threatening wind, casting Anna's bedroom in ever-changing shadows. She had opened the window to hear when Friedrich arrived to sweep her away.

Anna stared at the small bag on her bed that she had brought to Weimar. All the beautiful dresses still hung in her wardrobe. She had put on her country dress, the one in which her father had picked her up just less than two years before.

She went over to the secretary where her warm pelisse hung over the chair and put it on. With a sigh, she sat down on the chair and opened the secretary one last time, pulling out a paper, quill, and ink to begin writing a letter. After she was done, she folded it neatly, walked over to her bed, and placed it on her pillow. The letter bore Christiane's name. For a moment, she just stood there, staring at it, hoping that Christiane would understand and forgive her for leaving like this.

She exhaled with determination and pulled her eyes away from it. With a look over her shoulder at the bedroom door, she went over to the window and then peered down at the street below. Friedrich was already waiting for her, but he didn't look up at the window and instead scanned his surroundings cautiously.

Anna hurried over to her bed, blew out the candle, and grabbed the suitcase. Before she slipped through the door, she took one last look at her bedroom which had been her refuge for the last two years. She would miss its comforts, the secretary, and perhaps even some of the beautiful dresses but then she shook her head in fierce determination and left.

While it was no problem shutting her bedroom door quietly, making her way to the front door silently was another matter. The floors and stairs creaked in various places. A few times on her way down, she stopped and just listened intently, but the house lay quiet this deep in the night. When she made it to the front door, she carefully turned the key and pushed the door open slowly. Anna held her breath. It creaked so loudly that surely someone had heard her. However, no one came. And only a moment later, she began to breathe again, and it was the only noise she could hear. The house was still quiet. Without any more hesitation, she slipped out into the night, closing the door behind her faster than she had opened it.

Friedrich was waiting for her below the stairs. His face was hard to read in the dark. He took her suitcase without uttering a word, and then her arm to guide her into the darkness and away from the house. Before her father's house was completely swallowed up by the night, Anna looked back over her shoulder at it one last time. She let out a shaky breath and let Friedrich lead her along.

Morning was dawning. Anna was surprised to see the sunrise after yesterday's terribly cold, gray, and windy weather. It made the rundown inn on the outskirts of Weimar seem quaint in the early morning light. For a moment, she wondered if anyone in her father's house had noticed she was gone.

She glanced at the coach waiting in front of the shabby inn. The sun was rising in the East. It was almost time to leave. Friedrich stood beside her, the rising sun illuminating his face and everything around them.

Friedrich shot the coachman a quick look and turned to face her. He took her now gloved hands into his. "The coach will take you all the way to Strasbourg, with several stops in between, but lodging has been arranged for you along the way." He looked at the inn. "It might not be much, but you'll be safe. I have written to my cousin in Strasbourg. I trust her to take you to your village once you arrive in the city." Friedrich watched the coachman climb into his seat. "Anna, I—"

"I can never repay you for your kindness, Friedrich," Anna said, interrupting him.

"I wish you would not leave." He lowered his eyes to stare at the ground.

"I fear I feel the same, but I cannot stay." She studied Friedrich's green eyes and saw the same sadness she felt swimming in them.

The coachman cleared his throat loudly, and Friedrich shot him a quick look. He drew closer to her. "I meant to tell you... Anna, I cannot bear to see you go without telling you how I feel about you." With that, he suddenly pulled her even closer, cradled her face with his hands, and softly kissed her lips. He let go of her as quickly as he had kissed her and took a step back. Anna tried to focus her eyes, but the world had tilted. Friedrich. He had kissed her. She started to feel dizzy and grabbed his arm to steady herself. "Promise me that I will see you again," he said, his voice was husky and urgent. "Promise me, Anna!"

She found his face. "I promise you, myself, and the world that we shall see each other again," she said, feeling flushed. Friedrich nodded in satisfaction and smiled broadly back at her. With that, Anna walked past him to the waiting coach, trying to hide the smile that had broken out on her own face. Friedrich hurried after her and helped her into the carriage, bowing lightly as she climbed in. She nodded in gratitude. "'Til we meet again."

Friedrich shut the door and took a step back. "'Til we meet again," he said quietly. The coachman gave his command, and the coach jerked into motion. Anna leaned out the window to watch Friedrich slowly disappear into the morning glow.

Chapter 11

1805

Anna stood by the well with the bucket in hand and looked back at her grandfather, who sat in a chair right by the front door of the parsonage. He had dozed off and sunken back in the chair. It had shocked her, when she had gotten back home, how much he had aged.

She pumped the water and filled the bucket to carry it back to the house. When she walked past her grandfather, she put it down and draped an arm around his neck. He was startled awake and smiled when he saw her face. She kissed his gray hair softly.

"My dear child." He gently patted her arm. Anna smiled back at him and picked up the bucket. She left it in the kitchen and made her way upstairs to the small bedroom at the end of the hallway. Her mother's. When she entered, her eyes immediately fell onto the small wooden cross that adorned the wall against which the bed stood.

The beautiful blue and airy curtains let some light through the only window in the bedroom, dipping it into a hazy late afternoon light.

Anna walked quietly to the bed in which her mother lay propped up under a heavy, rough-looking blanket. For a moment, her eyes lingered on her mother's form. Then, they wandered to her drawn face. She feared what was inevitably to come. Her mother's health and her grandfather's age would mean that she'd be utterly alone in the not-so-distant future. She swallowed again, this time to down the fear that had gripped her suddenly, tightening her throat.

Anna stilled her trembling hand and placed it on her mother's forehead. Her eyes remained closed, but Anna caught her low mumble. She studied her mother's hair, which was wrapped in braids around her head covered somewhat by a cap. Her skin was pale like the light that came through the curtains, with dark shadows encircling her eyes. The tray with a small soup plate still rested on her lap, and the broth seemed untouched. Anna sat down on the bed beside her. She finally opened her eyes. "Anna!"

"You haven't eaten any of your good broth, Mama," Anna said, looking at the clean spoon on the tray.

"I'm not very hungry, child," her mother said weakly, turning her head away from the tray.

"It will give you strength." She picked up the spoon. "Please, Mama, you need to eat." She put some broth on the spoon and slowly guided it to her mother's lips. Anna continued to feed her a few more spoonfuls. Neither of them spoke. When her mother turned her head to the side again, Anna sighed and put the spoon back down on the tray.

"Not only your grandfather is glad you are back," her mother said weakly, turning back toward her with a weary smile. "Your aunt has been of great assistance but you, Anna... we truly missed you."

Anna returned her smile but then grew serious. "So, you're not angry with me?"

Her mother looked at her thoughtfully. "If he really is the gentleman you say he is, then I indeed wonder if it was wise to refuse him, child." Anna looked at the hands in her lap, the scar on her left thumb pad was now almost completely invisible. "I only wanted the best for you, Anna."

"I know that, Mama. I do." They both went silent and stared into the void. Anna knew her mother had meant it, but she nevertheless felt that she had disappointed both her and her grandfather.

Anna attempted to feed her mother another spoon of soup, but she shook her head vehemently. "Now tell me about this young man," her mother said with a soft smile.

"He is just as much a gentleman as Herr von Bendeleben but without the name, title, or fortune, of course," Anna said with a far-off look. She then told her mother everything about Friedrich: his work, how they danced together, about their day exploring Weimar and the area around the city. She felt excitement at finally being able to tell someone about him, but she also mourned the fact that she didn't know if she would ever see him again.

It was a mild summer's night when Anna sat beside her grandfather in front of the parsonage. Despite the surprisingly warm evening air,

Anna had a thin shawl wrapped around her shoulders. In her lap was a pair of breeches that she was mending. The flickering light of the lantern that hung by the front door made it difficult to place the stitches, so Anna would rest her eyes every few moments. Her grandfather was holding a large Bible and was reading to her from the Gospel of John, more from memory than from the faint outline of the words on the page.

He suddenly stopped and rested the big book against his legs. "He would have made a fine match, my girl."

Anna looked up at him and sighed inwardly. This wasn't the first time her grandfather had said it. "Marriage alone cannot make one happy."

"But it saves some from a broken heart." He looked at her over the rim of his glasses and then up to her mother's bedroom window. "And loneliness," he added.

"He still has not married her, you know," Anna said.

"So I hear. Living like this with a woman. I'm glad, child, that you left this house of fornication."

"Grandpapa!" Anna leaned forward toward him. "She's a good-hearted woman. And she loves him. She is practically his wife." She didn't want her grandfather to get the wrong impression about Christiane. She had been missing her terribly and felt she had to defend her.

The old pastor's face grew concerned. "But the heart of the affair is that she is not. Not without the blessing of the church." Anna fell silent. Of course, her grandfather was right.

They sat in silence for a moment. The sounds of the summery night filled the air. After a moment, Anna spoke. "Was it right of me to refuse Herr von Bendeleben, Grandpapa? He certainly would have made a good husband."

Her grandfather placed his weathered hand on hers. "Would you refuse to marry that Friedrich of yours you've been talking about ever since you returned… if he proposed?" Anna opened her mouth to protest, but how could she refute it. The pastor watched her carefully. Against her will, she couldn't help but break out into a smile. "I did not think so," her grandfather added with a raspy laugh. "And that makes you different from your father, even though I am certain he had his own reasons for not marrying Christiane or your mother all those years ago."

Anna searched her grandfather's face. This was the first time he had ever spoken so openly about her parents' past. She leaned forward, listening intently when her grandfather continued. "Your father did not want to settle down. He felt too young to get married. Look at the great poet and man he has become. And a playwright… and the many other things he is now."

Anna hung on every word, grateful for her grandfather sharing so openly. He turned to her fully, the Bible in his lap completely forgotten. "I have admired your father since the day I met him and invited him into my home. I knew straight away that I had the great pleasure of meeting one of the earth's greatest minds. Would he have become who he is if he had married your mother and settled down at such a young age, you think?" Anna knew that her grandfather did not expect an answer from her but hearing him speak about her father like that… he had never spoken of him in those terms. In awe and reverence. Her grandfather had only briefly paused. He went on with a far-off look in his eyes. "Your mother certainly was his muse back then. His poems attest to that. But would she still have inspired him to greatness years later? I hear that he has often enough looked for new… inspiration, shall we say?" Anna thought she caught a flash of disappointment in his eyes, but then he smiled at her with a nod and put his hand on her shoulder. "Anna, I do not think you are in any danger of becoming like him," he added reassuringly.

Anna knew her grandfather was right, but he didn't know everything about her. "I'm more like him than you think," she said quietly without looking at the old man. When she finally met his eyes, she could see his confusion. She hesitated and shook her head, but she knew it was the right time, and he was the right person to entrust her secret with. She put down the breeches she had been mending.

"I will be right back and then you will see. I will show you," she said and hastened inside the house. Her grandfather called after her, but she continued as if she didn't hear him, trembling with excitement and anticipation. She ran to her room and got her notebook and in a short moment was back at her grandfather's side.

"Ah, the notebook. You still have it then," he said with a smile. "I hoped for it to be of some use to you in Weimar."

Anna returned a grateful smile. "It was my steady companion. And still is." She swallowed and looked her grandfather square in the face. The notebook was in her arms pressed against her chest. She cleared her throat. "I write, Grandpapa."

Her grandfather clearly had not understood what she meant by those few simple words. "I know you do, child. Very well, I might add—"

"I've been writing poetry," Anna said hastily. "And plays. I have been working on a tragedy for months now." She looked at her grandfather expectantly, but he only stared at her. Anna was not sure what else to say, so she held out her notebook to him. He hesitantly and slowly took it from her. For a moment, it rested in his hands, and he neither looked at it nor opened it but instead studied her face. He finally turned his attention to the notebook and began to read. Turning page after page, skimming, trying to make out the words in the dim light. Occasionally, he would linger a moment longer on a page, his lips moving silently while he read. Anna could feel her palms getting moist, her stomach in knots. He was the first person she let read her almost finished play.

After what seemed like an eternity, he finally closed the notebook and searched her face intently. "It seems you take after your father after all," he said, deep in thought.

"I have been studying Greek, Grandpapa, and the Greek plays with August. He taught me what he learned from his tutor," Anna said, the words just tumbling out of her. "He—"

Her grandfather held up his hand and she fell silent. He studied her for a moment. With a bit of effort, he pushed himself up. When he stood in front of her, he looked determined. "You must return to your father," he said resolutely.

Anna jumped up in horror. "How can you say that? I belong here. I cannot go back. You said it yourself... that his home is a house of fornication. How could you want me to return there?" Anna was breathing heavily with a creeping terror. She could never go back.

"Sit down, child. You also seem to have inherited your father's temper." Anna sat down reluctantly, perhaps angrily. "You cannot learn anything more here. But your father's house seems to be a house of learning... among other things. He could teach you more than I ever could. Anna, you have a gift. You cannot stay here and let it go to waste."

"He does not know that I write," Anna said, her face hard.

"Then you will tell him," her grandfather said, putting his hand on her shoulder.

Anna looked down at her hands in her lap. She felt tears forming in her eyes and wiped them away with the back of her hand. "So you will send me back to him?"

"Nothing pleased me more than you returning to us. But life here is not your life, child."

"What about Mother?" Anna sniffled.

Her grandfather nodded knowingly. "I will take care of her. As will your aunt," he said gently.

Anna nodded sadly. How she would miss her mother again. "I'm not certain if I'm still welcome in his house. I left rather suddenly. And as you remember, I refused his friend." Anna swallowed at the thought.

"Let me write to him first. And now that Herr Bendeleben has married that French vicomtesse, as your brother writes, I am sure your father has forgiven you for not marrying him."

Anna turned to her grandfather, her eyes pleading. "Please do not tell him why you want me to return to Weimar. I feel I need to tell him so myself."

"Yes, I understand," the old pastor said kindly. He started for the house. "It is late. We should retire." He put his hand on her shoulder once more. "Even though you are more like your father than we all thought, do not make the same mistake and pursue your gift at the cost of love, child."

Anna patted her grandfather's hand on her shoulder. "You're truly wise, Pastor Brion." The old man smiled at the praise and went into the house. Anna looked at the night sky above, which shone dark blue. She didn't want to leave and return to Weimar, to her father, but she also knew, that if anything should ever become of her writing, she had to leave Sessenheim once more.

Anna was sitting by her mother's bedside, holding one of her hands. She sniffed back the tears and wondered if this goodbye was a little less heart-wrenching because she had done it before. The first time she had left, she hadn't been sure if she'd ever see her mother again. While still young, the sickness had taken its toll. Her cheeks were hollow and her skin paper thin and dry. However, since Anna had come back home, her mother seemed to have improved steadily and had looked quite well lately. Her face was a little more flushed and some of the color had returned to her lips.

She felt her mother's hand on her cheek and leaned into it. With her thumb, her mother wiped at the tears that ran down her cheeks. "Now, Anna. There is no reason for tears." Anna attempted a smile. It felt like a grimace. "I've gotten so much better. And we will write to each other, yes?" Anna nodded and wiped at her tears. "Now that's much better." Her mother smiled warmly. "Your grandfather is right, you know."

Anna threw herself into her mother's arms. "I will miss you so, Mama." She felt her mother choke back tears.

"And so shall I. And so shall I, dear child." She kissed her hair and stroked her head.

Anna knew it was time and got up. She picked up the bag standing next to her feet. "Goodbye, Mama. I will write to you soon. I promise."

Friederike nodded with a smile. "And so will I. Godspeed, my child."

Anna slowly walked down the stairs. Apprehension grew with every step. Outside, her grandfather was already waiting on his buggy to take her to Strasbourg from where she would take a coach.

"We better make haste. We don't want to miss the coach," her grandfather said. Anna nodded and climbed onto the buggy to sit down beside him. As they drove off, she turned to glance at the parsonage and swallowed hard. For a moment, she let her eyes linger on her mother's bedroom window, but then she turned around and looked ahead at the long winding country road. To the left and right of them, villagers were bringing in the harvest. Their songs reached her ear. She closed her eyes, took a deep breath to smell the air, rested her head on her grandfather's shoulder, and let the rattling of the buggy lull her to sleep.

Anna felt her grandfather's hand on her arm and looked up. He brought the buggy to a sudden stop. Ahead lay Strasbourg. Columns of smoke rose from the city, but not from its chimneys.

Several houses were smoldering, but the singular tower of the cathedral was gleaming peacefully in the dying sunlight.

"What do you think has happened?" Anna asked her grandfather, her eyes trained on the charred carcasses of houses.

"I'm not sure, but we shall find out soon." He clicked his tongue, and the horse pulled the buggy forward.

Moments later, they entered the city and saw a column of soldiers march ahead of them. "The French," Anna's grandfather muttered under his breath.

A shiver went up her spine. Napoleon's troops had reached Strasbourg. "Is it safe for us here?"

Anna could tell by the old man's narrowed eyes that he was assessing the situation. After a moment, he leaned toward her. His voice was low. "I heard a week ago that the Austrians have surrendered to Napoleon's army at Ulm. Now they're here. I suspect that occupying Strasbourg is just one of Napoleon's strategies to consolidate control and position his forces to further his campaigns. I don't think he means to harm the population or cause any meaningful destruction," her grandfather explained, throwing a side glance at the houses.

As they drove farther toward the center of the city, the streets became more and more deserted.

"Is it wise to continue to the coaching inn?" Anna asked, looking at the French soldiers they passed.

"Perhaps it would be safer to turn around and get to another coaching inn in another town," he said thoughtfully. "If I didn't have business to conduct in Strasbourg, I would have taken you to Haguenau straight away, anyways," he added. Anna knew her grandfather traveled on occasion to Strasbourg for church business and errands. Haguenau was closer and northeast of Sessenheim and located along the travel route to Weimar.

"What do you suggest?" For a moment, Anna wondered if her journey to Weimar would be sensible at all. If Napoleon intended to move his armies farther northeast, she would be caught on the same roads with them. "Do you think Napoleon plans to advance farther east?" she asked the old man.

"I think the French emperor has grander ambitions than simply defeating the Austrians and taking Strasbourg. The question is who will stop him," he said, his face lined with worry. "Let's turn around and make our way to Haguenau," he added with a look at the evening sun. Anna followed his gaze. It would be dark soon. "We will find lodgings for the night at an inn or tavern in one of the villages we passed through," he said as he turned around the buggy.

When they left the city behind, he smiled at her encouragingly, which calmed Anna. She completely trusted her grandfather's judgment. He was a sharp-witted and wise man.

The second village to the north of Strasbourg had a tavern with some rooms for rent. They arrived after nightfall, but the kind tavern keeper gave their horse a place in the barn and them a room. He even was so kind to serve them some bread with cheese to still their hunger after a long day of travel. While Anna needed to share a room with her grandfather, she was too exhausted to find any fault in that.

The room was small and had not been cleaned in a while. Her grandfather insisted on sleeping in the chair, even though she protested. He wouldn't hear of it. And after a short debate, Anna gave up and took the bed. She was too tired to win this argument. Without changing out of her dusty travel clothes, she lay down on top of the blanket. Her grandfather removed his boots and sank into the chair. Within moments, he snored loudly. After a few more moments, Anna drifted off into a fitful sleep herself.

After their night in the tavern, they traveled on to Haguenau. Pastor Brion had been correct in that they did not encounter any other French forces on their way there. They arrived at the coaching inn just in time. Anna only had a few moments for a short yet tearful goodbye with her grandfather, who reassured her yet again that her travels to Weimar should not be interrupted by any other possible French campaigns. She hoped he was right.

Anna kissed the old man's cheek. "Thank you, grandfather. I shall miss you."

"Not as much as I will, my child," he hugged her tightly and then let go. He cleared his throat and turned away to hand the coachman her bag. She said a silent prayer that she would see the old man again one day soon.

Anna had been traveling for two days when drums and marching jerked her out of her sleep. She was not the only passenger in the coach. Next to her was a young girl and across from her sat the girl's mother and older brother. They all looked in confusion at each other over the sudden ruckus outside. Anna peered out the window and saw columns of soldiers in blue and white uniforms marching along the road they were taking.

"French soldiers," she said, drawing back quickly and trying to keep the fear out of her voice so as not to frighten the young girl next to her.

"The French," the young man across from her spat, his hands balled into fists.

"Remain calm, Joseph," his mother hissed.

Anna listened nervously to the light and airy marching music played by flutes and the rhythm of the drums that hammered against her ear when the coach came to a sudden halt. Anna held her breath. The coachman opened the door and peered inside, his face grim. "We need to take another route." The mother wanted to protest but he was faster. "The French are advancing. We must outrun them." He slammed the door shut and moments later turned the coach around. Anna stared out the window, swallowing down her rising fear.

Chapter 12

1805

To her great relief, Anna had avoided the French for the rest of her journey and arrived in Weimar safely. The French army had not reached the duchy, but rumors of Napoleon's forces pushing eastward had reached the city.

Anna shook her head to disperse her worries and looked at her father, Christiane, and August chatting happily around the dinner table. She had been rather quiet but had to suppress a smile watching them. It was their first dinner together since her return. Anna had been afraid that they would not be as welcoming this time, but her fears had been unwarranted.

August, of course, had been overjoyed by her return. Her father had also been very obliging and seemed rather happy at her presence. And to her great relief, he had made no mention of Herr von Bendeleben. Christiane, however, had been reserved at first. August had told her that his mother had felt hurt by Anna leaving without a goodbye. But in no time, Christiane treated her like she always had, and it was soon as if she had never left. Even Erhart seemed glad to see her again. That had surprised her the most—along with the fact that he was still in her father's service. Another welcome news was that Geist had left her father's service, which she hoped would give her unrestricted and uninterrupted use of the library and its books.

Christiane, who sat next to her at the dining table, put a hand on hers. "I'm so glad you have returned to us, my dear."

Goethe smiled broadly at her. He leaned back in his chair and patted his stomach. "I cannot eat another bite. You have outdone yourself again, love." He looked at Anna. "Don't you think so, Anna?"

"It's very delicious indeed." She smiled at Christiane.

"Did you hear, Anna? The Prussians came through town. People say the French will pursue them all the way to Potsdam, if necessary," August's eyes were wide with excitement.

"Now, August. Let us not spoil a perfect dinner with the talk of war," Goethe said lightly, but Anna detected a hint of concern.

"But Father, Napoleon... the French will—"

"The French are not that bad, son," Goethe said, his voice stern. "Now *your* French, however," he added with a chuckle.

"I did hear some alarming news on my way to Weimar," Anna said. Everyone looked at her. "I saw them. On the roads. Early on in my journey and in Strasbourg. Columns of French soldiers," Anna added. August gaped at her with wide eyes. Then he shot his father a look that seemed to say 'I told you so.'

Goethe yawned. "It is late. I will retire early today. A full belly makes one tire rather prematurely," he said. Goethe stood and left the room with a warm smile in Anna's direction.

Christiane got up as well and then leaned in closely to Anna. August craned his neck to hear what his mother had to say, hoping for more news about the French soldiers, Anna presumed. "He has been in such a good mood since he received the letter from your grandfather that you wished to return," Christiane said.

August seemed to look a bit disappointed that there was no more talk of the French emperor or his army. He came over to them. "My Greek has gotten much better, Anna. Better than yours, I dare say?" August puffed out his chest. "I will show you tomorrow. We shall have a declension contest." He grinned broadly at her. "Father employed a new tutor for me. Herr Riemer is excellent. You will like him; we have become great friends. He can teach us both if Father allows. If not, you'll need to study day and night to catch up to my proficiency," he said with playful arrogance.

"Now, August. Leave your sister alone. It seems to me you're out to ruin her health."

Anna laughed and winked at August. "You know I like a good challenge, dear brother. I dare say I will be just as fluent as you by Christmas. Shall we see?"

Christiane huffed and rolled her eyes. She rang for the servant and began clearing the table while Anna shook hands with August, sealing their bet.

"We shall see, dear sister," August said with a smug grin before leaving the dining room.

Shortly thereafter, the maidservant entered and took over clearing the table. Christiane pulled Anna aside. In a low voice, she asked, "Have you been writing while you were gone?"

"I have indeed. The play is almost finished. I'm working on the last act," Anna whispered excitedly.

"It's time to tell your father. No more hesitations, Anna," Christiane's voice was soft but urgent.

"I will talk to him, I promise. When the time is right." She tried to ignore the lump that had begun to form in her throat. It was time to tell, that much she knew. She just hadn't figured out how to best do the telling.

Not only were her father, Christiane, and August happy she was back in Weimar, Friedrich was as well. She had sent him a letter as soon as the decision was made to return, and he had written back immediately to let her know that he was overjoyed. As soon as she'd known which day her father would be at court, she'd informed Friedrich. That morning, her father had left early, so Friedrich and Anna agreed to meet by the theater for a stroll and picnic in the park. It had been a dry and mild fall. Winter was coming in only a few weeks, and it was probably the last opportunity to enjoy good weather before the rains set in.

When Anna first saw Friedrich, waiting in front of the theater for her, he seemed changed. He no longer wore the tousled curls that she loved and seemed impossible to tame. His hair was shorter, and his curls had vanished. He also wore a new, very blue waistcoat and a high collar that made him look rather formal. From afar, she had not recognized him immediately. She wasn't sure if she liked this new Friedrich. He greeted her enthusiastically but rather stiffly. She took it in stride and excused it for having been apart.

They walked in awkward silence for the first little while. When they got to the park, they saw other couples out promenading. Most of the trees in the park had already begun to lose their leaves. The rich fat green of spring and summer had long faded. Friedrich had taken the wicker basket she had brought, and under his arm, he carried a blanket that he had brought. They walked toward the Ilm River, crossed a bridge, and came to a meadow. A house stood on the far side, and the area was deserted and quiet, save for the soft sounds of sparrows in the trees, the angry cawing of crows, and the distant calls of geese flying south. A gentle breeze stirred the fallen leaves, making them dance around. Anna took a deep breath, savoring the earthy scents of autumn.

"A perfect place," Friedrich said. He stopped walking, put down the basket, and squatted down to feel the grass. "It is dry." Anna took the blanket from him, unfolded it, and began to spread it out. "Let me help you with that," Friedrich said. Anna smiled shyly at him and together they spread out the blanket. He took her hand and helped her sit down. "I did not dare to hope you would return. You do not know how happy it makes me to see you, Anna," Friedrich said quietly as he sat down next to her. He looked at her with concerned eyes. "You seem rather quiet. I had hoped you'd feel the same."

Anna thought he sounded disappointed, so she smiled at him to give him some reassurance and try to overcome the awkwardness she felt and had not expected. "I am sorry. May I be truthful with you? I did not want to return to Weimar, but my grandfather insisted. He is a wise man, and it would be foolish of me not to heed him," she said. She realized that her words hadn't probably sounded encouraging to Friedrich, so she continued quickly. "On the other hand, knowing you would be here and that I would see you again, made it rather easy to return." She smiled confidently at him now, and Friedrich broke out in a grin of relief.

Anna pointed to the house that could barely be seen behind the trees. "Whose garden are we invading?"

Friedrich laughed. "Your father's."

Anna stared at the house, stunned. She had not known that her father owned another house.

"He used to live and work here when he first came to Weimar. The duke gifted it to him. He barely uses it now from what I understand, but he and the duke turned its gardens into this English park." Friedrich spread his arms. "Look at the trees they've been planting."

Anna followed Friedrich's gaze. "I've never seen these types of trees before, anywhere."

"Japanese Maple for one, from what I learned. And over there, that's a ginkgo tree. Your father has a fascination with them," Friedrich said and opened the picnic basket. Anna studied the trees for a moment. She would ask her father about them. "Let's see what you brought," Friedrich said, interrupting her thoughts. With a big hungry grin, he began to take out bread, cheese, and a few apples. "Let's eat."

"A very good idea. I'm famished," Anna said and helped him unpack.

She took some cheese and bread and laid it out before herself. Friedrich had leaned back on his elbows and watched her while chewing on a piece of bread. She looked at him with raised eyebrows, wondering why he was looking at her with such intensity. He cleared his throat and sat up, peeking into the basket to see what else it contained. "Now, what is this?" He pulled out Anna's notebook. "I hope you will not make me eat this," he said with a laugh.

Anna joined in his laughter but then grew somber. "I once made you a promise to share something with you." Anna motioned to her notebook in his hands.

Friedrich perked up. "I have not forgotten it." He studied her face for a moment but then turned to the notebook and opened it. Anna ate and watched Friedrich intently as he read silently.

"You do not mind me eating, do you? While you read?" Anna said between bites. Friedrich did not respond, so Anna assumed he agreed and bit into an apple.

Friedrich suddenly looked up at her. "I do not understand much about poetry, but your words are beautiful. Reading these... it's like catching a glimpse of your soul," he said deep in thought. He returned to reading in the notebook. Occasionally, he would shake his head but never took his eyes off the page. Without looking, he grabbed a piece of bread and tore into it with his teeth. "But your play. I *do* know plays. Anna! This is brilliant. Here, in the third act... these verses...," he said with his mouth full. He got up and after swallowing his last bite, he positioned himself in front of Anna like an actor. Anna giggled. He raised one arm theatrically and looked toward the sky. "'Fortuna lauds immortality's greatest prize.'" He lowered his gaze and locked eyes with her. "'A goddess's kiss without vile or vice.'"

"I now understand why you chose to become a carpenter," Anna laughed. But then she grew serious. "So, you think it is any good?"

Friedrich crouched down to be at Anna's eye level. "I do indeed. Anna, this is truly marvelous. You ought to get it published."

"I'm not sure I want that. And how... how would I do that?" she said, lowering her eyes.

"Your father! He can surely help you!"

"That would mean I would have to show him my writing first," she said quietly. Anna looked at the house. "He might not like it."

"Oh, he will, Anna. Be assured," Friedrich said, biting into a piece of cheese and nodding vehemently.

When they had finished their lunch, they walked leisurely back to Weimar. Anna put her arm through Friedrich's. On her other arm, the empty basket was dangling. It had been a wonderful afternoon. They had talked and talked. She no longer felt awkward around him, and Friedrich no longer seemed so stiff. It was as if they hadn't been apart at all.

Chapter 13

1806

Goethe sat in one of the parlor's armed chairs and carefully studied Friedrich, standing before him in his Sunday best. The young man nervously let his hat run through his fingers in circles. It annoyed Goethe, but he tried to ignore it. "Now, speak frankly," Goethe demanded.

Friedrich ran one of his hands through his hair. "I... I love your daughter, sir." Friedrich's eyes dropped to the floor.

"And does she love you?" Goethe asked nonchalantly.

Friedrich stepped forward. "Yes, yes, she does, sir!" He seemed to notice his forwardness and straightened his shoulders, his voice calmer. "I will be a good husband to her, be assured, sir." Friedrich looked him straight in the eyes.

Goethe regarded him carefully for a moment and then cleared his throat. "Do you want to marry her simply because she is *my* daughter?"

Friedrich seemed perplexed. "Oh, no, sir! I have loved Anna long before I knew she was your daughter. I loved her from the moment you introduced her to me in the theater, and she listened to me rattle on about the carpentry of the set."

Goethe pursed his lips, trying to read Friedrich's face, but he could not detect any ill intent. He already knew him as an upright young man, and he hadn't seemed any different today when he had asked for an audience. He clearly loved Anna. But Goethe couldn't help himself. After all, the father of a young woman should never make it easy on any of her suitors. "And now that you know Anna is my daughter, you do not see any reasons why you shouldn't marry the daughter of Johann Wolfgang von Goethe?"

Friedrich's eyes narrowed. He stepped forward yet again and with straight shoulders said determinedly, "With all due respect, sir, it is not you or her family I wish to marry. Neither do I believe that marrying for one's station is superior to marrying for love." He cleared his throat. His voice was a low rumble now. "Anna has my heart, sir, to love her through the eternities. She has my body to protect and care for her and my soul to give her comfort and companionship as long as I shall live. She makes me want to be a better man. And I mean to make her happy, sir, as she makes me."

Goethe wasn't often at a loss of words. The young man's forwardness and declarations of love were indeed reassuring. Yet, they did not make up for the fact that he was not the kind of match he had intended for Anna.

Goethe sighed and stood without looking at Friedrich. He walked over to the window and with his back turned to Friedrich, he said: "Understand my hesitations, but with your current work... how

will you provide for my daughter? You do not have much to offer."
Goethe turned around to face Friedrich. "I cannot let my daughter
marry a carpenter. You must see that." Friedrich hung his head, his
eyes fixated on the tip of his shoes. "We must find you a position at
court," Goethe said thoughtfully. Friedrich looked up at him, hope
dancing in his eyes. "No. That will be impossible," Goethe said, deep
in thought. Friedrich looked devastated again. "But... I'm sure the
duke would allow me, his minister, to appoint someone to run the
theater for me. I'm away far too often, and when I am here, it takes
up too much of my time."

Friedrich stared at him wide-eyed. "But, sir..." It would ensure
an adequate pension, Goethe thought to himself. "I have no such
experience," Friedrich continued, interrupting Goethe's thoughts.

"Oh, you do." Goethe walked over to Friedrich. "You know how
the theater is run. You wouldn't need to worry about the direction
of the plays or the actors... Demoiselle Christiane seems to be able
to deal with that unruly lot quite well." He studied Friedrich's
perplexed face. "What do you say, young sir?"

Friedrich was still gaping at Goethe. "I... I did not come here
to—"

"I know. But you must see that I cannot allow you to marry my
daughter with only the income of a carpenter."

"Then I will accept your offer graciously." Friedrich bowed to him
lightly. "You have my word that I will take care of your daughter. In
every way possible. I will not hold her back from becoming a writer.
And maybe someday, we could see if her play—"

"Her what? What is this about?" Goethe was stunned.

Friedrich cleared his throat uncomfortably. "She has not spoken with you."

"About what?"

"I think you should ask Anna that."

"I'm asking you," Goethe said impatiently.

Friedrich eyed the door as if he wanted to escape. He sighed and looked at the older man. "Anna... she is writing. Poetry. Plays. She is very talented, sir. You must read her work."

Goethe stared at him in utter disbelief, then abruptly said, "Please, you must excuse me now."

Friedrich hesitated. He opened his mouth but then let it go and walked over to the door. Before he left, he turned around and bowed to Goethe.

Goethe stared at the closed door. His daughter was writing. How could he not have known? He went back to the window and watched people go by. It helped him think, but then his eyes found the three small ginkgo trees that he had ordered to be planted alongside the square. He squinted to watch the leaves sail to the ground in the fall breeze. These intriguingly shaped leaves. He had been fascinated with these trees since his time in Italy. His thoughts turned to Anna. He didn't know if he was angry at her secrecy or proud that she had taken up the pen. He needed to see for himself.

Anna sat across from August at the table in the library. She was chewing on her lip and kept her eyes glued to the page, writing as quickly as she could. August across from her did the same. She ignored him so as to not be distracted by him or Herr Riemer, who was pacing up and down alongside the table with his hands locked behind his back. He occasionally came over and glanced over their shoulders, making little satisfied grunts and giving the occasional sigh. It was mostly when he looked at August's work that he sighed, Anna noticed, which encouraged her all the more. She had to see to it that she beat August.

A few moments later, Herr Riemer cleared his throat. "Are you nearly finished?"

"I am indeed," Anna said and put down her quill. She let out a long breath and examined the writing on the page in front of her. In satisfaction, she nodded to herself. August, however, grunted grumpily and continued writing in haste. They had agreed to see who could translate a passage from Aristotle's *Poetics* the most accurately in a given hour. "I promised you I would catch up on my Greek by Christmas, my dear brother," she teased. She folded her arms and leaned back in her chair, unwilling to give up tormenting August just yet. "Oh, wait. But it is not even close to December yet." She sent a big grin in his direction.

Herr Riemer laughed heartily. "I had the hope, Master August, that with your sister so eager to study Greek, you would be inclined to press on with your studies." Herr Riemer winked at Anna, and she laughed as well. Poor August, Anna thought and ceased laughing. She didn't want to tease him too much.

August put down his quill with a huff. "I'm finished. That is all that counts, is it not?"

Anna wanted to respond, but the door flew open. Everyone froze.

In the door frame stood Goethe. His eyes found Anna and rested on her for a brief moment, his face unreadable. Anna felt the blood drain from her face. August and Herr Riemer exchanged a quick look. Anna swallowed and slowly stood, carefully closing her books and folding the paper.

Her father turned to his son and Riemer. "Leave us. I must speak with Anna," he said, his voice stern.

Herr Riemer and August left the library without a word. Once the door closed behind them, her father came over to her. "Please. Sit!" he said. Anna sat back down slowly. She swallowed and chewed on her lip, but this time it was not because of Greek. Her father looked at her books. "I was not made aware that you had joined August's studies. I must increase Herr Riemer's salary since he seems to tutor not one but two students."

Anna didn't know how to respond. What was best to say, now that she had been found out? She'd known it was only a matter of time until her father got wind of it. She felt her stomach bottom out and lowered her eyes to stare at her hands in her lap. Her fingers were stained with ink as they always were, and she now wondered why her father had never noticed it.

Goethe started pacing around the table, his eyes locked onto her. When he reached the corner of the table where Anna's notebook lay, he stopped pacing. He stared at it for a moment and then with a glance at her, picked it up. She held her breath and noticed she was kneading the scar on her thumb.

When he opened the notebook, Anna drew in a sharp breath. He began reading silently, scanning page after page. All the while, his face was expressionless. Eventually, he closed the notebook and looked at her.

"Why do you hide this from me?"

Anna's heart sank and she lowered her eyes again. How could she possibly respond? She regretted waiting to tell him. She had promised her grandfather and Friedrich. Why hadn't she told him?

"I will keep this," her father said, holding the notebook up to her. She wanted to protest and opened her mouth, but he held up his hand. This was the very reason she had hesitated to tell him. That he would take her notebook away from her.

He went to leave, her notebook in hand, but turned around to her once more before exiting. "Right after breakfast tomorrow, you will come to my study. I will instruct you myself for two hours every day after breakfast from now on." Anna stared at him, her mouth open. "Do not be late. I'm a rather busy man as you know." He left and closed the door quietly behind him.

Anna fell back in her chair. Had she heard him correctly? She shook her head. He would instruct her, he had said. In what, she suddenly wondered. Greek? Certainly not. Writing? Oh, how she hoped it to be writing. She gathered up her things and left the library as well, sorely missing her notebook.

Anna and Christiane made their way through the backstage of the theater. Today, it lacked the busyness and crowdedness that Anna had experienced on her first visit. Very few people were about. In the far back was a group of carpenters working on a stage set that looked like a group of trees. Not far off, she saw Friedrich painting wooden panels. He hadn't noticed her yet and seemed focused on his task. His face was as tense as the muscles in his right arm that held the paintbrush.

Christiane led Anna to a group of actors, who were just coming in through a backstage door. They were not in costume and held bottles in their hands. Christiane sighed. "I do not understand why your father prefers that I be the one to talk some sense into these people." She sighed yet again, this time more loudly. "Yet it is obvious that it has to be done. Your father always says that they need to take lessons from the likes of Friedrich. Or from the painters and sculptors." Her face became stern and determined. She turned to Anna. "Go on and speak with Friedrich," she said, thrusting her chin in the direction of him. "I will come to you when I'm finished speaking to this lot." Anna gave Christiane a quick nod and headed in Friedrich's direction.

When she was almost by his side, he looked up and his eyes found her. He broke out into a smile and put down his paintbrush. "This surely is a pleasant surprise," he said, wiping his hands on his leather apron.

Anna returned his smile. She was happy to see him, but even more so because she finally had the chance to speak with him. There was so much news to share. "Christiane has to speak with the actors, so I came along. In... in hopes that I would be able to speak with you," she said, the words tumbling out of her. She took a breath to slow down. "And I was hoping to ask you if... if you have spoken with my father," she added shyly, trying not to swallow her words.

Friedrich stepped closer to her. "I have indeed. Did he not tell you?" Friedrich asked, face scrunched in concern.

"No. He did not." Why hadn't her father mentioned it to her? "Now, will you tell me what he said? I'm dying to hear it."

Friedrich nodded. He cast his eyes around and then pulled her with him farther away from the group of carpenters. His face was serious when he turned to her. "Your father offered me a position to run the theater for him. He thinks that I would not be able to support you otherwise," Friedrich said in a hushed voice.

"So, he agreed?"

"I'm not sure he did," Friedrich said with a far-off gaze.

"What do you mean?" Anna tried to make him look at her again by placing her hand on his cheek and turning his head gently toward her, searching his eyes.

"Once I mentioned that I would not stand in your way of writing, he dismissed me rather abruptly... without giving me his consent and us his blessing." His eyes lingered on Anna for a small moment, studying her face carefully. Her brows furrowed and her stomach dropped. "Anna, it appeared he did not know anything about your writing. Have you not spoken to him about it?"

Anna bit her lip and turned away from Friedrich, taking a couple of steps to the side and away from him. She could feel Friedrich's eyes on her back. Without turning back around to face him, she said, "I did not. But he found out today when he came into the library." Anna lowered her eyes and for a moment studied the hem of her dress before she continued. "He took my notebook and told me that he himself would instruct me from now on." Anna turned back around to Friedrich and straightened her shoulders. "Isn't that wonderful, Friedrich?" She forced a smile. But where would that leave them?

"I suppose it is," he said haltingly. He came over to her and placed his hands on her upper arms. "But what about us, Anna? What about our plans?"

Anna wiggled herself out of Friedrich's grip and stepped around him. "You will need to talk to my father again."

"This is not what I meant—"

"Tonight! Tonight, he will come to the theater. Talk to him then. Demand an answer."

Friedrich did not seem to share her enthusiasm. His face was lined with worry. "I don't know. Here at the theater?" He started pacing. "I don't know if that would be wise."

"Why wouldn't it be?" Anna asked defiantly.

"Anna! Come, Anna!" Christiane was calling out to her.

"I have to go," Anna said quickly to Friedrich. She looked at Christiane, whose hands were on her hips, looking in her direction impatiently. "Tonight, Friedrich. Let us not wait any longer," she added, stepping close to him and hastily brushing his cheek with a kiss in hopes no one would notice. She knew he needed the encouragement. Without another word, she hurried off, feeling that Friedrich was staring after her and realizing that he hadn't bid her goodbye.

When Goethe approached the group of actors backstage, he grunted to himself in satisfaction. He had known that Christiane would manage well dealing with them. They looked put together, were already in costume without him having to shout at them to get changed, and there was no alcohol to be seen. Goethe clapped his hands twice loudly. "Everyone on stage for the rehearsal! At once! Now!" The actors scurried away. Goethe followed them until he heard someone approach him from behind. He turned around and faced Friedrich.

"A word, sir?" Friedrich asked, looking determined.

Goethe's brows furrowed. "Can't it wait?"

Friedrich shook his head vehemently, more to himself, Goethe thought. "About yesterday, sir. When I came to your house to—"

"Ah! The position." The young man was eager to accept the offer he had made him. Of course, he was.

"No," Friedrich said. "Anna. Do we have your blessing, sir?"

Goethe's face turned stern. "Marriage is not in my daughter's near future," Goethe said coldly and sidestepped Friedrich to head for the stage. He felt Friedrich stare after him. Anna needed to focus on her writing for now. Marriage and children would only interfere with her ambitions. Domestic duties would be an unnecessary distraction. How would she find the time to write? And then there were the dangers of childbirth. She had an intellect and a gift he had not yet seen in a woman, and he would not stand by idly to see it go to waste.

In his study, Goethe was standing in front of one of the ancient busts he had acquired while in Italy. His eyes had been lingering on it for a while, but his thoughts were turned to Anna's writing and the guidance he could give her. After all, she was a woman. Any attempts to pursue a literary career would be frowned upon by society. He had to find a way for her to share her writing. Perhaps a nom de plume—

His thoughts were interrupted by the abrupt opening of the door. He whipped around and saw Anna, breathing heavily and standing in front of him. She had stormed in without a knock. No one ever entered his study without his permission. Despite the anger he felt rising in him, he quickly collected himself. "Anna! I'm glad you're here. I—" A look at Anna's face stopped him. Her eyes burned with rage. Both of her hands were balled up in fists, and her stance seemed to indicate that she could pounce on him any minute. He had never seen that side of her.

"I will marry Friedrich without your consent. I do not need your blessing. I am a grown woman, and I'm not sure I care much for your blessing anyway, Father." She spat out the last word.

It took him a moment to collect himself after her outburst. He felt his jaw clench. "It would be foolish to marry that carpenter. He has no prospects. And he will hardly be able to feed you or your offspring." He was shocked by the coldness in his own words.

"I do not care about these things," Anna said with a raised voice.

"Oh, you will. When you are cold and hungry with rain leaking through your roof, you will remember my words."

"He works very hard. He will earn his living."

"And what will you do? Take care of your home and the ten hungry little mouths clinging to your skirts? You won't be writing, Anna. I promise you that." He saw her flinch and knew he had gotten to her.

"I would give it all up for him, for a family of my own," Anna gave back.

He stepped closer to her and continued more gently. "You cannot simply cease to be who you are, Anna. It is not possible. Writing is part of you."

"*He* is part of me."

She was infuriatingly stubborn. How she reminded him of himself back in the day. He thought of his father, who had died years and years ago, and how he had defied his wishes. But Anna was a woman, and it was her duty to obey him.

He noticed her glance at her notebook on his desk. "You had no right," she said and stormed over to grab it.

"He's your muse, is he?"

"No, you were, Father," Anna said, barely audible. She turned around and walked out of the study with her notebook, leaving Goethe to stare after her.

Anna had remained in her room for days, refusing to come to dinner and desperately avoiding her father. She hadn't seen him in nearly a fortnight, and Christiane grew more concerned about their dispute and the effect it had on everyone in the house with each passing day. Anna bit her lip at the shame she now felt for having burst into her father's study like that. While she harbored some regrets over the words she'd had with him, she was also still angry with him at his refusal to give Friedrich and her his blessing. Today, a letter from Friedrich had arrived. He had requested to see her. She knew they needed to discuss the matter and decide on their next course of action. This afternoon, she would slip away to meet him.

Anna and Friedrich sat on a bench under a tall oak tree in the park. Its leaves had already turned a reddish-orange hue but seemed to want to hang on, refusing to shed. Its colorful and grand canopy provided the refuge Anna had hoped they would find in the park, which had become her favorite place on the outskirts of the city. Friedrich was holding her hand in silence while they listened to the rushing of the nearby river and the low rumbling in the distance, indicating a storm was brewing. She had told Friedrich about her quarrel with her father. He had silently listened, growing more concerned with each passing minute. Now, they both sat in silence.

"We shall be married by the end of the year," he said suddenly. Her heart jumped, and a lump in her throat started to form. "I shall speak with the pastor presently," he continued with his eyes locked on the horizon. But then he turned to face her. He quickly scanned their surrounding and then placed a hand on her cheek. His face drew nearer, and before Anna could utter a word, she felt his warm lips on hers. She felt herself blush instantaneously, and when he withdrew, she lowered her eyes. He lifted up her chin so she would look at him. "If that's what you would want," he said gently.

She swallowed the lump in her throat and smiled. "Yes." He let go of her and smiled in relief. She wondered if Friedrich had thought about where they would live after they had wed. Would they stay in Weimar?

Her thoughts were interrupted by a thunderous explosion. Not close but near the city. It was not thunder.

"That was not the storm," Friedrich said, echoing her thoughts. He jumped up and reached for her hand. "That was a canon blast." He pulled her with him. They needed to make haste and get home before the French entered Weimar.

They broke into a run. When they reached the first buildings, people rushed past them. Some pulled carts with their belongings stacked high, and others carried large bundles. They hurried in the direction from which Anna and Friedrich were coming. Toward the river and away from the city.

"The French will take Weimar quickly," Friedrich said, looking around, his face dark with worry.

Anna drew closer to him, holding onto his arm more tightly. A woman rushed past them. Anna reached out and caught her by the arm. "Tell me, good woman. Are the French entered the city?" Anna asked, her voice thick with urgency.

"They're at the city gate," the woman said between breaths. "The French are here." Her voice was shrill now and her eyes wild. She tore away from Anna's grasp and hurried away. Anna stared after her, terror paralyzing her mind and body.

Friedrich wrapped his arm around her protectively and craned his neck in all directions. "I must get you home at once." He pulled at her, but Anna stood rooted in place. "Now, Anna! We need to make haste!" Friedrich seized her arm and dragged her along. The commotion in the city increased with every corner they rounded. Panic had gripped people everywhere. There was shouting in the far distance. The rumble of cannons as well as the firing of muskets drew nearer. Anna shuddered but stumbled half running, half walking with Friedrich through the streets of Weimar toward her father's house.

When they finally reached the house, the square in front was deserted. Fear surged within her. They reached the front door, and Friedrich took Anna by her arms, turning her to face him. "You'll be safe at your father's house. He is well known, even among the French. They would not dare... They admire poets. They admire him." He hammered against the door. "I will leave you now," he said, scanning the square and streets beyond.

"Where will you go?" Anna asked, her voice shrill with panic.

Before Friedrich could answer, the door swung open. "Thank goodness! Anna!" Christiane breathed in a hushed voice. She pulled Anna inside. "You better hurry home. Take the back alleys!" Christiane urged Friedrich before she hastily shut the door.

Goethe stared into the dark of their bedroom, trying to make out the pictures that hung on the opposite wall. Only when a flash of light from the outside lit up the room could he see them. Christiane lay next to him. She wasn't sleeping either. She jumped slightly and her fingers dug into his hand every time there was shouting in French, the celebratory firing of a musket, the breaking of glass, or a woman's scream.

He shot up when he heard the crashing of wood downstairs. Christiane drew her breath in sharply and covered her mouth with both hands to muffle her scream. They had broken down the front door, he realized, fighting against the terror trying to paralyze him. The sounds of boots and French voices echoed up to them. Christiane grabbed his arm, but he freed himself from her grasp and got out of bed.

For a moment, he listened intently. He heard furniture being thrown around and glass breaking. He grabbed his breeches and banyan and got dressed in a hurry. Ignoring Christiane's frightened breathing, he was about to open the door when a woman's scream downstairs split the air. "Anna!" Goethe ripped open the door and stormed out.

But Anna stood right outside his door in front of him, clad in her nightgown, trembling in fear. There was another scream from downstairs and Anna jumped. He realized the scream belonged to the maidservant. Goethe put his finger on his lips, motioning for Anna to remain still and quiet. A door behind them opened and August stepped out, fully dressed, his lips pressed into a tight line. Goethe signaled to him to remain where he was.

The French voices grew nearer and louder as boots stomped up toward them. Goethe looked at Anna and August, trying to figure out the best course of action, but his mind was blank. He wasn't sure what horrified him more, that he couldn't form a thought or the approaching soldiers. But then, as by instinct, he shoved Anna back into her room right when the French soldiers appeared at the top of the stairs, their muskets with bayonets attached drawn and on the ready. Their uniforms looked filthy, and greed and violence swam in their wild eyes. It made him shudder.

The soldiers spotted him and August in the semi-dark and aimed at them. Goethe threw out his left arm to shield August, who had staggered backward. Christiane came rushing out of their bedroom, clad in nothing but her nightgown. She stepped right in front of Goethe. Frozen by shock, he stared at her back. The muskets were now pointing at her chest and belly. "Leave! This instant! How dare you!" Her voice held no fear.

The French soldiers smirked at each other. One went over to Anna's bedroom door and kicked it open with his foot. Anna came into view, her eyes wide with terror, hugging herself. "*Allez, Mademoiselle!*" He said. She staggered backward. Quick as a weasel, he went inside the bedroom and grabbed Anna by the wrist.

"No!" August shouted.

Goethe raised his fist to the soldier. "Leave her! She's my daughter! Do not dare to put your filthy hands on her!"

The second soldier pointed his musket at Goethe again and came toward him. Christiane stepped in front of him once more, the bayonet only centimeters from her heart. Goethe stared at her in utter disbelief. *Woman, what are you doing*, he thought in a mixture of awe, anger, and fear.

"You will regret your intrusion," Christiane yelled. "This is Monsieur Goethe! How dare you enter his house like this! Your captain shall hear of this." She was fuming.

"Monsieur Goethe?" The soldier looked clueless and just shrugged, still pointing his bayonet at Christiane. The other soldier let go of Anna and came over to his comrade. He started whispering something in his ear, all the while both of their eyes remained fixed on Goethe. A realization seemed to dawn on the soldier with the bayonet, and without another word, they went down the stairs and exited the house.

They all sighed in relief, except for Goethe, who had turned to Christiane. "You have the nerves of Napoleon himself, woman." He shook his head in disbelief and started down the stairs. August followed him. "Go back to bed and stay in your rooms. Please!" He said over his shoulder. Christiane guided a visibly shaken Anna to her room and put her to bed.

The day was dawning already, and the early morning light seeped through the shutters. Goethe had lit a candle and left it burning for the remainder of the night. Everything was still and quiet outside. The French soldiers had gotten drunk and were now sleeping off the night's debauchery somewhere. Here and there, he heard a dog bark, and birds began to greet the day. Goethe lay next to Christiane. Neither had been able to sleep after the terrible events of the night. He took her hand in his and turned to her.

"You have always been by my side," he said, looking at her face that was lined from the night's terror. "Today, I will make arrangements to wed you, Mademoiselle." Christiane stared at him in disbelief, utterly speechless, but then she broke out into a broad, beaming smile. "We should try to get a little bit of sleep at least. Good night, Frau von Goethe." He blew out the candle and then squeezed her hand. He could hear her think, but she didn't utter a word.

She simply shifted her body closer to his. "Good night, Herr von Goethe," she said, her voice hoarse with happiness.

Goethe was dressed in his best waistcoat. He ignored the disarray and broken glass around him in the parlor and regarded the French general sitting across from him. The Frenchman's German was excellent, his immaculate uniform impressive. The general's tricorne hat rested on his right knee. Goethe noticed how shiny his boots were, surprising in times of war and considering the havoc caused by him and his soldiers across the city and in his own home.

"Please accept my sincere apologies, Monsieur Goethe. In times like these, etiquette is overlooked far too often," the general said in his French accent.

"I believe your soldiers have never known any etiquette, even in times of peace," Goethe replied. "There's nothing worse than aggressive stupidity, General," he added.

"They are common soldiers. They long for their wives, French wine, and France. I will personally see to it that your door is repaired."

"And my servant?" Goethe said grimly. The general shrugged and wanted to respond, but Goethe was in no mood for French platitudes, and he wasn't finished giving him a piece of his mind, no matter the man's rank or authority. "War is in truth a disease, General, and—"

Before Goethe could finish his sentence, the door swung open, and Anna was bringing in tea and coffee. Goethe could tell that her hands were slightly trembling. The general stood, clicked his heels, and bowed to Anna. She curtsied in return but did not hide her mistrust and disdain for the man.

"You have a very beautiful daughter," the general said, looking over the rim of his cup at Anna.

"Indeed." Goethe thanked Anna with a reassuring smile as she handed him his cup of tea.

"I must say, it is a great honor to make your acquaintance, Monsieur von Goethe. Your genius is hailed all over France. Our emperor has read your *Werther* numerous times," he said admiringly.

"I did not know Napoleon favored reading. He seems rather occupied with expanding France's borders and—"

Everyone jumped when someone came rushing in. It was Friedrich, out of breath and looking around wildly until his eyes found Anna, and he bent over in relief. Anna burst into tears when she saw him. Friedrich strode over to her and took her in his arms. "Are you alright? I heard that the French—" He cut himself off when he spotted the French general, his face darkening. The general seemed to enjoy the scene before him.

Not Goethe. He got up. "May I inquire why you chose to invade my house like this?" But no one answered his question.

Goethe watched with furrowed brows as Anna took Friedrich's hand and pulled him with her. "Friedrich was only concerned about my safety, Father. Please excuse us," she said over her shoulder before shutting the door behind them. Goethe stared after them.

"Young love," the general sighed in a way that said, 'What can you do?'

Goethe still stared at the door. "General! I cannot accept any delay in the repair of my main entrance!"

The general got up with a smirk. "I will see to it this instant." He put on his tricorne, clapped his heels, and bowed to Goethe. "It has been a great honor, Monsieur Goethe." He saluted him.

"I thank you for your visit," Goethe said absentmindedly and accompanied the general to the broken front door. Outside, two of his soldiers were waiting for him to take him to his carriage. Before stepping through the doorway, still littered with debris, the general turned around to face him.

"Congratulations on your engagement." The general must have noticed Goethe's confusion because he explained. "I heard you're marrying the woman who so easily wanted to give her life for yours."

Goethe was stunned. "How—?" He fell silent at the general's smug expression. Weimar's administration was in French hands now, and the French were known to establish networks of spies and informants in their conquered territories. Goethe was one of Weimar's most prominent citizens. Of course, the French would know about his every move and his visit to the parish church earlier that morning.

Chapter 14

1806

The pale autumn sun rose in the East and fell through the windows of the church, bathing its interior and the few souls in attendance in a warm glow. The pastor made the sign of the cross above Christiane's and her father's heads, blessing the union he had just sanctified. Anna smiled at the happiness dancing across Christiane's face.

Christiane wore a simple off-white dress with a beautiful silk shawl wrapped around her shoulders. August was beaming at his parents. They were now a true family. She was happy for August whose parents' union legitimized his birth. Anna put a hand on her belly in an attempt to dissolve the knot that had formed in her stomach. Her birth would forever remain illegitimate.

Her father cleared his throat. "I would like to share a poem I have written for Frau von Goethe for the occasion." Everyone looked at him in surprise as he pulled out a piece of paper from the inner pocket of his waistcoat. He turned to face Christiane and began to read:

"*Found*"

Once through the forest
Alone I went;
To seek for nothing
My thoughts were bent.

I i' the shadow
A flower stand there
As stars it glisten'd,
As eyes 'twas fair.

I sought to pluck it,
It gently said:
"Shall I be gather'd
Only to fade?"

With all its roots
I dug it with care,
And took it home
To my garden fair.

In silent corner
Soon it was set;

There grows it ever,
There blooms it yet.

Anna felt Friedrich's hand brush against hers. He gently touched her fingers and she smiled. Her father handed the paper to Christiane, and she pressed it against her bosom, her eyes moist. How simple yet so beautiful of a poem her father had written for his new bride. Anna wiped at her eyes. She felt Friedrich squeeze her hand.

Her father and Christiane left the altar and walked past the few attendees down the aisle toward the church door to exit. The pastor and everyone else followed them. No church bells rang, however, as was usually the custom. The happy union was not announced to the city. Her father had insisted so. Reluctantly, the pastor had obliged one of Weimar's most famous citizens.

Outside, the married couple and the few guests shook hands with the clergyman. A few members of Christiane's family, her maidservant, August, Herr Riemer, Erhart, Friedrich, and Anna had been the only witnesses to the ceremony. None of Goethe's friends and family were there.

Their small procession made their way back to the house under the cover of the dawn's early rising for a celebratory meal that had been prepared by servants and Christiane herself the previous day. The city lay still as they walked in happy silence. Here and there, remnants of the looting of Weimar by Napoleon's troops a few days prior were still visible, but they ignored it. Though Anna knew the invasion had brought sorrow in abundance, a small part of her couldn't help but recognize the blessing that had come alongside it. Without it, Christiane would have remained as unwed as ever.

A few days after the wedding, Anna and Friedrich told her father that they had secretly gotten married. Without his blessing. The shock was written across Goethe's face but he met the news with utter silence. He only flinched when they told him they would be leaving Weimar and settling in Strasbourg, close to her mother and grandfather.

The decision had not been easy for Anna. She felt as if she was betraying her father. As if she had chosen Friedrich over him. But her father had left her no choice. He had not approved of Friedrich nor their wish to get married. They had to leave Weimar. It had been difficult to accept that she would never have the opportunity to be instructed by him, to never partake of his vast knowledge. Friedrich had encouraged her to continue writing and had convinced her that she was capable of doing so without her father's help.

Anna looked up at the house she had called home for the past few years and then at Christiane and August. She put down her small bag and tightened the shawl around her shoulders. Sniffing back the tears that were running down her cheeks now, she went over to Christiane and embraced her tightly. August's face was somber as he looked on, his lips tight.

"Please. Do write," Christiane sniffled, pressing Anna even more closely to her bosom.

"I shall miss you dearly," Anna choked out.

Christiane let go of her and took her by the hands. Anna felt Christiane's thumb caressing the small golden wedding band on her right ring finger. Christiane glanced at Friedrich. "He seems to be a good man. May he make you happy, Anna."

Friedrich came up to them. He had overheard her words. "That I shall. You have my word, Madame." He put an arm around Anna and led her gently toward an old horse he had managed to get from his uncle. It carried a couple of bundles.

"Wait," Anna said. She pulled free and walked over to August, whose eyes were glued to the ground while he kicked around a small rock with the tip of his shoe. From underneath her shawl, Anna pulled out her notebook and handed it to August. "Will you give this to him?"

"But—"

"Please." August stared gravely at the notebook in his hands. Anna proceeded to give August a quick hug. "Goodbye, August." She let go of him and walked over to Friedrich. Anna let him help her onto the mount and soon after, he led them away from the people and house she had called home.

Her father had not come to bid her farewell. Anna turned around and saw Christiane drying her face with a handkerchief. August slowly raised his hand in a goodbye. She answered his kind gesture with a nod and looked straight ahead. Once they had rounded the corner, her tears fell without inhibition, the overwhelming loss twisting her stomach into a big knot.

Goethe pulled the blanket up to cover his shoulders. It was rather cold in their bed chamber tonight, and he involuntarily had to shudder. Christiane stood barefooted with her back to him, taking off her dressing gown. When she turned around, his eyes fell on the bulging stomach underneath her nightgown. He shuddered again.

"I cannot believe you let her go," Christiane said accusingly while climbing into bed. Her cold feet touched his and he shivered yet again.

"She is a grown and married woman now. What would you have me do? Lock her in her bedroom? Her new husband would hardly appreciate that."

"You could have given them your blessing, and they would have stayed. You had promised Friedrich that position." Christiane was now almost shouting at him. "Everything would have turned out alright but for your pride and stubbornness." She turned around in a huff and with her back toward him, pulled the down blanket away from him.

For a moment, he stared at her back in silence. Then he said quietly, "She didn't care for my blessing." Christiane did not react. He wondered if she had already fallen asleep. She was always very tired when pregnant. "She is throwing away her future. She cannot be a wife, a mother, and a writer," he continued, not caring if she was already asleep or not.

"How will you know that?" Christiane mumbled.

"Just look at Frau von Stein. Her poems... She would have been a great poetess. But her marriage and her numerous children have never allowed her to write more than a handful of good poems."

To his surprise, Christiane broke out in laughter and turned around to him. "Herr von Goethe. I would not attempt to compare Anna and Frau von Stein in any manner whatsoever. They are as much different as you and me. If Anna had married Herr von Bendeleben, I would have thought her to be as vain, indifferent, and shallow as Frau von Stein." Christiane sat up, pushed back the blanket, and put both of her hands around her protruding belly. "Since Anna came to live with us, she has been studying in that library of yours at every possible moment. She had your son teach her everything he learned from his tutors. Still, she did as you had asked and worked hard to help me run this house. She is not in any way like Frau von Stein. She is your daughter. And she has inherited your gift," Christiane added more gently, searching his face in the semi-dark.

Goethe sighed audibly. "Indeed she has." Goethe knew Christiane was right, of course. And he had felt nothing but regret to not have given Anna and Friedrich his blessing, to let her part without reconciling with her.

Chapter 15

1807

Anna pulled her legs closer to her body, the straw from the mattress poking through and into her side. She had a woolen cloak wrapped around her body with a heavy coarse blanket on top of her, but it did not suffice. The cold had crept in so far as to hold her insides in its icy grip. Only half conscious, she blew into her stiff fingers and looked around the small attic bedroom that Friedrich had been able to secure for them. It was dimly lit by the cold moon that shone through the small and only window. She could make out the white clouds of breath that escaped her mouth in the semi-dark. The bed and one chair standing in the corner right next to where the knee attic wall sloped down was all they had been able to acquire. She dozed off, thinking of warm bread by Christiane's kitchen stove.

She dreamed of Friedrich, coming into their attic bedroom through the creaking door. He looked tired and very thin. He undressed quickly and quietly and with only his shirt on, slid into bed with her. When she felt his cold body against hers, she knew it wasn't a dream. He put his arm around her and gently stroked her stomach. She found his hand to let him know she was awake.

"Sleep, Anna. I did not mean to wake you," he whispered in her ear, his warm breath brushing up against it.

"How was work at the theater?" Anna asked.

"It is the same work everywhere."

She could hear the weariness in his voice and drew him closer. "You're as cold as ice." She rubbed his hand and then his arm that still rested on her belly.

"If it gets any colder, I will have to buy some wood to heat this room. I am sorry about all of this, Anna. You deserve all the comforts." He stroked her belly again.

"All that counts is that we are together. And I am only a few hours away from my family. We need to be grateful to your friend for finding you work at the Strasbourg theater. It is a blessing."

"Someday, I will build you your own house. One just like your father's."

"Absolutely not. That house is too big and too much to bear," Anna protested.

"I meant his garden house, my dear, in the park in Weimar," Friedrich said between quiet laughs. "Do you remember it?"

"Yes, I remember," she said quietly and heaved a silent sigh. It stung to think of the park and Weimar.

"What do you say? If it gets any colder, we just move into the theater," he said teasingly.

Anna giggled. "I think they would notice." But then her thoughts turned to her mother and grandfather. "Can we visit my mother and grandfather once the weather has warmed?" She stood in desperate need of their company. Friedrich worked much, and she was alone often. She tried to occupy herself with reading and had even dabbled in some writing, but she longed for good conversation.

"We shall take you as soon as the snow is gone," he promised. "You may spend a good few weeks in the countryside with them. It will do you some good," he added and gently stroked her stomach again. A few minutes later, his hand stilled, and she knew he had fallen asleep. Soon winter would be over, and she would get to spend more time in Sessenheim with her mother and grandfather. As Anna drifted off to sleep, she thought of the fields and pond near her grandfather's parsonage. The thought instantaneously warmed her.

Goethe held up the manuscript for all to see. He made eye contact with the actors either sitting on chairs or standing around him. They all held some pages of papers in their hands and watched him expectantly. "You were assigned your parts last time. Today, we shall begin our rehearsals."

The actors nodded in excitement. Some began to talk amongst themselves, nodding to each other enthusiastically.

"A superb play, if I may say so, sir," one of the actors said.

Goethe smiled proudly. "You may so indeed."

Another actor stepped forward. "Sir, will you not act in your play again?"

"I will not. And it is not my play," Goethe said.

Everyone quieted down and looked at him in surprise. A couple of actors whispered among themselves, pointing to lines on the pages they held.

"Who is the playwright then?" the same actor asked.

Goethe started to walk across the stage, turning his back on them. He sighed deeply and then turned back around to face them. "The playwright is my daughter."

"You have a daughter?" one of the actors blurted out.

He ignored their gasps and stares and cleared his throat. "Mademoiselle Anna is my daughter, and she has written this play."

"A woman has written this?" one of the carpenters asked.

Goethe narrowed his eyes. "Why would a woman not be capable of writing a play such as this?" The carpenter lowered his eyes and took a step back.

One of the actors came toward him. When he stood in front of him, he grinned. "She seems to take after you, sir."

"Thank you," Goethe said. He cleared his throat again. "Enough flattery now. Let us rehearse."

Anna was quietly pacing back and forth in their small attic bedroom. Occasionally, she stopped at the window and craned her neck to get a glimpse of the street below. But it lay quiet and deserted. She stared at the letter in her hand and at the door, wishing Friedrich would come home. The minutes dragged on. She couldn't wait to speak with him. Sometimes, she wished his work as a carpenter at the theater wouldn't keep him so late. Especially tonight she wanted him to be home with her.

She walked over and smiled at the little bundle in the cradle. With a smile, she very gently touched the little fuzz of her daughter's hair, peeking out from underneath her bonnet. She let her eyes linger on the baby's peaceful sleeping for a moment. Looking at her, she had never felt happier or content in her life. The only time she had come near to feeling this happy was when she was writing.

She carefully pulled her hand back when she heard someone come up the stairs. Friedrich. He was home. Moments later, the door creaked open, and Friedrich slipped in. She noticed again how very tired he looked.

Anna couldn't wait. She went to him and held up the letter to him. "This came today. From Christiane," she said in a hushed voice.

Friedrich looked puzzled but he took the letter from her. Anna walked over to the bed and sat down on its edge. Friedrich went over to the cradle across from her and lovingly gazed at their daughter they had named Friederike, then came over to her to sit down beside her. He began reading the letter, whispering every word aloud.

"'My dear, Anna! How glad we have been to hear the good news of the birth of your child. One can only hope that she has not inherited her grandfather's looks.'" Friedrich chuckled lightly and Anna leaned in to look over his shoulder at the letter in his hands. He continued reading quietly. "'Anna, I must inform you that a fourth child was born unto us. Again, it has not been our good fortune to see the child live.'"

"Good heavens—" Friedrich said loudly. He, along with Anna, glanced at the cradle, but everything seemed quiet, so he continued.

"'Oh, Anna, how I miss you in this time of sorrow. Your father has left Weimar and I'm in need of a friend. Won't you come to visit me? I must introduce myself to my granddaughter. Please come at once.'"

Friedrich let his hand holding the letter sink down. "I dare say this news is grave." He got up and went over to the cradle.

Anna followed him, put her arm around his waist, and gazed at their daughter with him. "It is indeed," she whispered.

Friedrich turned toward her. "You should go. With your father gone—"

"She's still so little. It's such a long journey. And how could we afford—"

"We can. With you gone, I could take on extra work. People always seem to need a carpenter," Friedrich said.

Anna pulled Friedrich away from the cradle. "But you work too much already," she said. Friedrich's health hadn't been the best for some time now.

Friedrich took her in his arms. "Christiane needs you. And it will be good for you, too, to spend some time with her and August. I know how much you've missed them. And she wants to meet her granddaughter. Don't worry about the little one. She's strong and healthy."

Anna smiled at Friedrich and hugged him, resting her cheek on his shoulder. "You are a perfectly good husband, Friedrich Lorenz," she said, smiling into his shirt and taking in the musky smell that made her feel at home.

"You are very agreeable as well," Friedrich teased. He pulled free and took her face in his hands to kiss her gently on the mouth. "I shall miss you both."

After several days of traveling and overnights in coaching inns, both Anna and little Friederike were exhausted. When they finally arrived in Weimar, Anna was relieved that their arduous journey had come to an end. She was surprised at how happy she was to be back.

With little Friederike cradled in her left arm and her travel bag in her right hand, she walked to her father's house. Once the house came into view across the square, she felt her throat tighten. The house lay peaceful in the evening light. Erhart had already lit all the lamps and the warm glow from the windows was inviting. In her arm, the baby was soundly asleep.

When she came to the door, Anna put down her bag to raise her fist to knock, but let it sink down soon after. She looked over her shoulder. The square lay quiet behind her. She hesitantly raised her hand again and knocked. The motion shook the baby awake and her loud wail echoed across the square. The door flew open and Christiane's beaming face greeted her.

"Oh, Anna!" She embraced her as much as she could with Anna holding the baby in her arm. Christiane pulled back and clapped her hands. "Oh! Is that... is that her?" Christiane took the baby from her and held it close. It stopped fussing immediately and Anna had to smile. They went inside, Anna following Christiane and the baby with her bag, glad to be home.

In the parlor, Anna watched Christiane sit down on the chaise longue and cuddle with the baby. After a few moments, Christiane looked up at her. "I'm so grateful you came," she said, her eyes watery.

"I was not certain I was welcome," Anna said, looking around the room. It hadn't changed in the least.

"You're always welcome. And your father is gone, Anna." Christiane got up and rocked Friederike, who had just woken up and began to fuss a little. "You will regret to hear that he took August with him," Christiane added. Anna swallowed down the disappointment. When she sighed, Christiane said, "Your brother misses you dearly, let me assure you."

"As I do him," Anna said with a look out the open parlor door toward the stairs, which led to where her bedroom had been. "I will stay at the coaching inn," she added.

"You will do no such thing!" Christiane held the baby protectively in her arms, pressing her tightly against her chest. "Your father will be gone for another month, maybe even two," Christiane said reassuringly. "And he would not mind. I know he wouldn't. He misses you, too, Anna."

"I find that hard to believe. He has never written to me since I left," Anna said. She hated that she felt resentful toward him but couldn't help it.

"He would never admit his wrongs. He is a proud man. Wouldn't you agree?" Christiane eyed her carefully. "If I may be so bold to say... I hope that someday you will find it in your heart to forgive him."

"It is not about forgiveness. If he cannot accept my marriage, I do not see how we can ever reconcile."

Christiane frowned. "You are much more like him than you know, dear," she said quietly, her voice flat. She studied Anna's face for a moment and looked as if she had more to add but hesitated. After a short pause, Christiane straightened her shoulders. "Anna, your father has published your poems. And he is putting on your play."

Anna fell back a step. Her head spun. "He—he did what? How could he! He—Without my permission? How—how dare he!" Her voice cracked with shock and anger.

Christiane's eyes narrowed. "Do forgive me, Anna. But I do not understand why this upsets you so. Is that not what you wanted?"

Christiane looked perplexed. Anna did not want to appear as an impertinent child or ungrateful, but why didn't Christiane see why this would upset her? "That is not what I wanted. I wanted his approval. His blessing. Not his connections," Anna blurted out.

"Oh, Anna! I did not think this would trouble you so." Christiane came over to her, shifted the baby to her left arm, and wrapped her right arm around Anna. "Let us talk of happier times. Please." Anna breathed in deeply to calm herself. After a short moment, Christiane let go of her. Shaking her head, she said, "I believe you look rather thin." With that, she pulled Anna with her out of the parlor toward the kitchen.

In the hallway, Anna stopped her. "I will stay until he returns and then demand my notebook back from him."

"Agreed, but first, we need to feed you. You are all bones, my dear," Christiane said and took Anna's hand once more. Anna wanted to protest but Christiane cut her off before she could utter a word. "I insist!"

Chapter 16

1807

There was a knock on his study's door. Goethe grunted what sounded like a 'come in' and continued reading. Someone entered, and he tore his gaze away from the book. "Anna!" He jumped up when he realized it was her, his chair almost tumbling over. He stepped around the desk to greet her. How pleased he was that she had come, even if it was unannounced. Christiane had written to him that Anna had come to Weimar to keep her company, but that she had stayed at the coaching inn as soon as she had heard that he was returning home.

"Please. Sit. Make yourself comfortable," he said, gesturing toward the chair in front of his desk. But Anna just shook her head. Her expression was stern, and he felt a pang of disappointment. This was not a pleasant call, he thought and swallowed. But he decided to not give up so easily. She was here and this was his opportunity to make amends. "I am glad you came to Weimar. It was kind of you to keep Christiane company. She had missed you so."

"And I missed her," Anna said flatly. There was a moment of silence, and when he was about to break the awkwardness between them, Anna cleared her throat and continued. "I'm here for my notebook. It was a mistake to leave it in your hands. If I had known that you would—"

"Anna! You do not understand. Your writing... you have a gift. An exceptional gift. I could not watch you throw it away," he said quickly to reassure her.

"You had no right!" Anna snapped. Her hands were balled into fists. Goethe took a step back, but she closed the distance between them. "I want you to stop the production of my play. Immediately!"

He backed away from her but then crossed his arms in defiance. He scrutinized her face. "Tell me this, Anna. Have you been writing since you left Weimar?" He uncrossed his arms and tried to soften his demeanor. "There's so much to learn. I can teach you all I know." He was pleading with her now.

"I have a daughter. I'm a wife. I write when I have time to do so," she replied defiantly.

"I had feared as much!" He bit his lip and instantly regretted his words. Over the years, he had learned to control his sharp tongue, but he still failed on occasion.

"You have no right!" Anna turned around and stormed out of the study. It took him a moment to collect himself, but then he went after her. In the hallway, he saw Anna take the baby out of Christiane's arms and vanish through the front door. His wife looked crestfallen. Tears swam in her eyes. He wanted to vanish like

Anna. Christiane shook her head disapprovingly in his direction and left for the kitchen, letting him stand there to stare at the closed door.

Anna sniffed back the tears as she was packing her bag in the small bedroom at the coaching inn. Her coach was leaving early in the morning, and she wanted to get everything ready for the long journey home before going to bed.

The door to her room was open. In the threshold stood Christiane, dressed in a warm redingote and quietly watching her. Voices and laughter echoed up at them from below. Little Friederike lay on top of the shabby old blanket that covered the old wooden bed, cooing and gurgling. After a few moments, Anna was done packing the few belongings she had brought.

"I wish you would stay just a little longer," Christiane said.

Anna didn't look up. "I have been gone too long already," she said, closing her bag. She then turned and saw Christiane crying quietly. Anna walked over and hugged her. "You are a dear friend. And I am glad I came." Anna let go of her and pulled out her handkerchief to hand it to Christiane. But when she looked back up, Christiane held something out to her as well. Her notebook!

"He wanted me to give it to you," Christiane sniffed. Anna stared at her notebook in Christiane's hand. "Don't you want it back?" Christiane asked. Anna just nodded and took it. She ran her hand over the familiar grooves in the leather. He had returned it to her. Her notebook. Anna pressed it against her chest and then walked over to the bed. She opened her bag and placed it carefully on top of her clothing.

The candle on her nightstand was almost burned out and soon the small, shabby room she had rented in the coaching inn would be in complete darkness. Friederike was asleep in her arms. Anna tried to focus on her quiet little breaths to drown out the muffled noises seeping in from downstairs. She looked at her bag and wiped angrily at the tears that stained her cheeks.

After lingering on it for a moment, she carefully got up and placed Friederike in the middle of the bed and then pulled the blanket over her little sleeping body. She walked over to her bag, pulled out the notebook, and walked back over to the bed. Before sitting down, she opened it and a letter fell out and glided to the floor. She stared at it and the name of the addressee that it bore. With another glance at Friederike to make sure she still slept soundly, Anna bent down slowly and picked up the letter. Her suspicious eyes fell on the beautiful signature on the bottom of the unfolded paper. It was signed by her father. She finally sat down on the bed, careful to not disturb the baby, and began to read.

Goethe walked to the theater's entrance hall, scanning the many faces in the crowd, who were greeting each other and talking, waiting for tonight's performance. When they noticed him, some greeted him, and others bowed. He barely acknowledged them. He locked his eyes on those still coming in from the street, but she was not among them.

Goethe wasn't ready to give up. She could still make it. He hoped and prayed that his letter had softened her heart and that she had changed her disposition toward him. He was good with words after all. Good enough that she would forgive him? And accept his blessing that he ought to have bestowed a long time ago? Doubts began to cloud his mind again.

He grunted in satisfaction at the throng of attendees, the excitement in their voices echoing in the beautiful vestibule crowned by a dome ceiling. Performances in the Weimar theater were always well attended. And an air of mystery had surrounded tonight's performance, which had not only intrigued regular theatergoers but had gripped the whole of Weimar.

He noticed his friend Frau von Stein enter. She merely nodded her greetings as she passed others as if she had neither the time nor the desire to engage with them. Right behind her, the duke and duchess and their entourage followed. People parted for them as the Red Sea. As they passed through, men bowed and women curtsied. Goethe went down to them and bowed himself, but then the duke took Goethe's hand and shook it, as he always did. They were old friends and Goethe felt a stir of gratitude once again for the duke's friendship and patronage. The duke could count on his loyalty for the rest of his days. Goethe proceeded to kiss the duchess's hand, greeted Frau von Stein, and then personally led them to their boxes. The crowd followed and the entrance hall emptied quickly.

After getting his guests settled and ordering the torches on the stage to be lit, Goethe hurried back to the vestibule where Friedrich was already waiting for him. The entrance hall was now almost void of people, except for a few latecomers who hastened into the theater. Goethe had written Friedrich months ago, informing him of his intentions to have Anna's play staged. He had sworn him to secrecy until he would have the opportunity to personally reveal the good news to her. When he had asked him in his latest letter to come to Weimar for the play's premiere, he was relieved that Friedrich had agreed to come.

Goethe shook the younger man's hand heartily and whispered something into his ear. Friedrich gave a quick nod. Together, they watched the entrance to the theater for a few more moments, but with each person that entered and with each passing second, Goethe grew more worried. With a last glance at the entrance, he ushered a similarly worried Friedrich to his box. The performance could not be delayed any further with the duke and duchess in attendance.

Goethe scanned the rows of chairs and then the boxes above. The audience held their breaths in anticipation. He spotted Friedrich seated next to Christiane and August. One seat next to them was still empty. Goethe swallowed down the disappointment. Perhaps Anna had never found his letter in the notebook. Christiane had assured him that she had delivered it to her. But perhaps Anna had decided to commit the letter to the fire upon finding it. He took a deep breath to quieten his mind. He saw Friedrich glancing at the double doors, but then the curtain rose behind him and the beautiful, picturesque ancient Greek town his carpenters had worked on came into view. There was a collective gasp from the audience.

Goethe cleared his throat and took a step forward. "Your highnesses, lords, ladies, and gentlemen, it is my good fortune and my great pleasure to introduce tonight's play *Archelaus*, written by my own daughter." Some members of the audience audibly drew breaths. Others began whispering to each other. Goethe noticed the duke leaning forward in his box. The duchess whispered something in his ear behind her fan with a side glance at Goethe. He had expected nothing less.

But none of that mattered a second later, because his eyes were drawn to the entrance, and there she stood, in an effortless red gown he had never seen her wear. She seemed transfixed. Her eyes were locked on the stage or him, he wasn't sure. Friedrich must have followed his gaze because he was up in an instant and left his box to make his way to Anna. When he appeared by her side, she appeared stunned and then overjoyed to see him. He quickly whispered something to her. She stared again at the stage, and Goethe motioned her forward. Anna lowered her eyes, embarrassed, and began walking towards him down the center aisle. As she arrived at the steps leading to the stage, Goethe took her hand, leading her up and to the center stage.

On stage, Goethe stepped aside and let Anna take her place at the center. He lifted an arm and held it out in Anna's direction. "Your highnesses, lords, ladies, and gentlemen, with your permission... It is my great pleasure now to welcome tonight's playwright to the stage." He smiled proudly at her, and she returned his smile.

Someone in the audience began to clap, and slowly, others followed suit, but not all. The citizens of Weimar would not welcome her so easily. The applause quieted down quickly, so he continued. "This is my daughter, Anna. She not only is a very talented playwright but also a fine poet." He looked at Anna, who now smiled at him without hesitation. "Let's proceed with the performance. Enjoy tonight's debut," Goethe added. He took a quick bow and then led Anna off the stage.

Backstage, Goethe faced Anna. Actors in costume and some of the crew gathered quietly around. Some bowed to her. She smiled , entirely taken aback by the respectful reception.

Goethe clapped his hands twice. "Places, everyone." The gathering dispersed and hurried away, some to the stage. Goethe stepped closer to Anna. "I am an old fool, Anna. Too proud to admit I have done you much wrong." He breathed out a long sigh.

"I am just as proud. I am the one who needs to apologize. You were right, I have acted childishly and stubbornly." She somberly avoided his eyes.

"I am still that way, so Christiane tells me." He laughed lightly at his own words, then grew serious. "I hope you can forgive me."

She looked up and studied him for a moment, then finally spoke. "Under one condition." He nodded for her to proceed. "If you can forgive me first."

Goethe took her hand and kissed it. He then embraced her. After a moment, he cleared his throat, let go of her, and kissed her forehead, ignoring the tears that swam in his eyes, obscuring his vision. "You better join your husband. You do not want to miss your own play, do you?" Anna smiled at him broadly and gently squeezed his hand. With another look at him, she hurried off the stage.

In the theater box, during the last act, Anna couldn't help but smile to herself. She couldn't remember a day she had ever felt so gratified and rewarded. To hear her own words infused with life by the actors, to hear her voice captured in their dramatics. It had taken her breath away. From this day forward all she would ever want to do was write. For the first time in her life, she felt proud of herself and immense gratitude for the gifts she had been given. She breathed in slowly and deeply, savoring the moment, making sure she felt it in her bones.

Anna looked at the stage. The final scene. She held her breath. One of the actors was stretched out on the ground. Dying. Another was kneeling by his side. The older man, in his anguish, turned to the younger with his right arm pointing to the heavens. "A father's love, considered a great blessing from above, shalt not cease in death."

The younger man covered his sorrowful weeping with his hands. A moment later, he took the older man's hands and placed them on his own head. "Fortuna lauds such love. Your blessing, Father, a guiding light I sought." The old man's hands slid down, and he died. The curtain slowly dropped.

For a moment, there was utter silence. Anna felt Christiane's hand squeeze hers lightly. She felt Friedrich go stiff next to her, but then he began clapping. Slowly, the audience joined him and then erupted in fervent applause. One after another, spectators leaped to their feet, even the duke and duchess rose from their seats and turned toward her, clapping ecstatically.

Her father appeared on stage, beckoning for her to come down. Anna exited the theater box and as she passed them, the audience rose in a standing ovation. Even the Duke and Duchess took to their feet. Voices cheered. The audience had erupted in 'bravos' as she walked down the aisle. But Anna only had eyes for her father. He was beaming at her. Her heart swelled and tears of joy began to obscure her vision.

On stage, Anna, Goethe, and the actors stood in a sea of flowers and laurels, bowing repeatedly to the thunderous applause. Anna smiled at Goethe. She sought Friedrich in their box, his face was beaming as well. August tipped his hat to her, and Christiane had tears streaming down her face. Anna's composure hung by a thread.

When the applause had died down and people began to exit, Anna could no longer hold back. She turned to her father. Goethe looked at her with raised eyebrows. "What is it? You look concerned."

"Please, Father, your truth," she implored.

"My truth?" He seemed puzzled.

"Your opinion, Father, on the performance of my tragedy?" Anna asked, trying to remain patient.

He studied her face for a moment and then took her hand. "Anna, it is a stupendous tragedy. Aristotle would be proud. You bestowed a profound sense of humanity upon Archelaus. Thus, you have earned profound respect, especially from the actors... and, if I may, the theater's director," he said with a wink. "You are a fine writer, my daughter. This is the truth, my truth, Anna. And don't forget that poetry is truth." He held out his arm and she took it, leading her off the stage and to the entrance hall where Friedrich, Christiane, and August awaited them.

They greeted them enthusiastically and heaped their praises on Anna and Goethe. But even though he had directed Anna's play, he gave all the honor to her.

When they filed out of the theater, Goethe turned to her. "I will see you home now," he said. Anna looked puzzled from him to Friedrich and back. "Friedrich has to see to the closing of the theater. This is his duty now," he added.

Friedrich grinned at her. They would be able to stay. Here in Weimar. Her heart leaped. A look at Christiane and August told her that this was the most welcome news. But then her face fell. She turned to her father. "But, Papa! I can hardly move back into my old bedroom."

He laughed heartily. "Who says you have to?" He nodded at Friedrich conspiratorially. "You may take up residence in the garden house if it pleases you." Anna stared at her father and Friedrich in disbelief. She then threw herself into her father's arms. "You shall be happy there, my child," he whispered in her ear.

Epilogue

Anna put down the quill and rubbed at the ink stains on her fingers in vain. She leaned back in the chair and examined the heap of papers on the secretary in front of her. Her eyes drifted out the open window in front of which she sat and gazed at the endless green of the park beyond the house. She let the light warm breeze brush against her face and closed her eyes for a moment. Then she heard her daughter's squeal followed by laughter. Before she could stand up to look outside, Friedrich came in, wearing just his breeches, boots, and a white unbuttoned dress shirt. She smiled at the tousled mess of hair on his head. He leaned down and kissed her hair. "Your father is here," he said with a twinkling in his ever-so-green eyes.

"I heard," Anna laughed. "I'll be right out." Friedrich nodded with a smile and left. Anna walked over to the bookcases lining the wall. She searched for a moment and finally found what she was looking for. She pulled out the book and read it on her way over to the secretary. For a moment, her eyes lingered on the open page, but then she put the book down and picked up her quill again. "Poetry is truth," she mumbled as she wrote, biting her lip in concentration. When the breeze from the outside carried children's laughter with it, Anna got up and leaned forward toward the open window to catch a glimpse of the joy below. With a smile, she put down the quill and left the study.

A Note from the Author

Dear Reader,

Thank you so much for reading *The Poet's Daughter*. I hope you liked it. Readers like you are everything to authors, and I would really appreciate it if you would take the time to leave an honest review on Amazon—just scan the QR code below. Reader reviews matter a lot. Other readers will appreciate hearing your opinion on the book—and of course, your feedback is very useful to me as I embark on my next books.

Warmest Regards,

C. K.

Selected Bibliography

Boyle, Nicholas. *Goethe: The Poet and the Age*. Vol. 1, 1991; Vol. 2, 2000. Harvard University Press.

Faust, Albert B. "On the Origins of the Gretchen-Theme in *Faust*." *The German Quarterly*, vol. 45, no. 3, 1972, pp. 341–349.

Goethe, Johann Wolfgang von. "Gefunden" [*Found*]. Translated by E.A. Bowring, 1813. *The Poems of Goethe*, edited by Eric A. Blackall, Princeton University Press, 1989.

Goethe, Johann Wolfgang von. *Dichtung und Wahrheit* [*Poetry and Truth*]. Translated by John Oxenford, 1849. Penguin Classics, 2009.

Goethe, Johann Wolfgang von. *Goethe's Letters to Friederike*. Edited by K. S. Guthke, 1972. Modern Language Association, 1983.

Goethe, Johann Wolfgang von. *Sessenheimer Songs. Goethe: The Collected Works*, edited by Eric A. Blackall, Princeton University Press, 1989.

Goethe, Johann Wolfgang von. "Willkommen und Abschied" [*Welcome and Farewell*]. Translated by Edgar Alfred Bowring. *The Poems of Goethe*, edited by Eric A. Blackall, Princeton University Press, 1989.

Guthke, Karl S. *Goethe and Schiller's Weimar: Essays on the Intellectual History of Eighteenth Century Germany*. 1972. Cambridge University Press.

Renker, Cindy, and Susanne Bach, editors. *Women from the Parsonage: Women Writers in 18th and 19th Century Germany*. Peter Lang, 2018.

Acknowledgements

This novel grew out of a screenplay I wrote over fifteen years ago. Like my other novels, this one, too, was a set of moving images in my mind; however, this one was a full-fledged feature film. The opening scene in the screenplay (and in my mind) was a bird's-eye view tracking shot, as they are called, in which the camera moved through Goethe's house in Weimar — seamlessly traveling through various rooms to showcase the layout of the poet's house and the actions of some of the characters in the different rooms. At the end of this opening scene, the camera spotted Geist and tracked him on his way to the front door where Erhart was handed a letter.

Last year, I decided to turn the screenplay into a novel. Parts of the aforementioned opening scene made it into Chapter Three. While *The Poet's Daughter* originated from a screenplay, there's one person whose teaching ultimately inspired it. I already mentioned my background on Goethe in the Preface, but I have yet to mention Hans-Wilhelm Kelling, my favorite professor whose class on Goethe

I took as an undergrad. I later was his teaching assistant for that same course where the first ideas for this story came to me more than twenty years ago. I want to thank him here for all he taught me, about German cultural history and of course, Goethe.

Next, I would like to thank Shaun and her team at The Book Whisperer for all their help and guidance in the production of this book. Without them, this book would not exist in this shape or form. Shaun's enthusiasm for this story, stemming from her own love for everything theater was the encouragement I needed to pursue the publication of this novel. Perhaps one day it will play out on screen as it did in my mind so many years ago. I would also like to thank Ayden at WhalesEdits for her helpful insights and suggestions, my designer at GetCovers who again made sure to capture my vision and be on brand, and PolishMapping for the useful map to provide some geographical guidance to my readers. It truly takes a village to bring my stories to you.

A big shoutout goes to my alpha and beta readers. What would I do without you?

And as always, I want to thank my family and friends for their support and encouragement without which I wouldn't and couldn't continue this writing journey.

About the Author

C. K. McAdam writes historical fiction. She holds a Ph.D. in Interdisciplinary Humanities and teaches college. Together with her family, she resides in Texas but hails originally from Germany where she grew up. In her free time, she loves to travel, hike, read historical fiction, play pickleball, spend time with her family, and go on walks with her corgi Merlin.

Subscribe to the author's newsletter by visiting **www.mcadambooks.com** for more info, giveaways, news, and updates.

Connect with the author on social media and don't hesitate to leave reviews. Every author appreciates them very much.

amazon.com/author/ckmcadam

instagram.com/ckmcadam

facebook.com/ckmcadam

twitter.com/CK_McAdam